Erin shout a downpour, "We need to get out of here."

With the conditions worsening by the moment, Matt didn't argue. He'd been searching close to one wall of the ravine and turned to head back to the trail.

"Do you need help?" Matt yelled to her. He took one step in her direction before water surged over the edge of the ravine in every natural depression. Cascading down and filling the gully floor, it raced toward them. Matt's heart stopped and he could barely breathe as he lunged toward Erin with his hand outstretched.

Erin glanced at the flash flood, back at Matt, her eyes wide with terror. She reached for his hand. Their fingers touched.

The narrow ravine forced the flash flood into a wall of water bearing down on them.

Matt wrapped one arm around a boulder and grabbed Erin's hand with the other. But his strength couldn't match that of Mother Nature.

"Erin!" Matt's bellow evaporated within the roar of the flood as Erin disappeared into its depths.

RESOLUTE SECURITY

LESLIE MARSHMAN

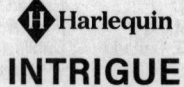
INTRIGUE

If you purchased this book without a cover you should be aware that this book is stolen property. It was reported as "unsold and destroyed" to the publisher, and neither the author nor the publisher has received any payment for this "stripped book."

MIX
Paper | Supporting responsible forestry
FSC® C021394

This one's for Joan, because I love a good villain.

Harlequin INTRIGUE™

ISBN-13: 978-1-335-69035-7

Recycling programs for this product may not exist in your area.

Resolute Security

Copyright © 2025 by Leslie Marshman

All rights reserved. No part of this book may be used or reproduced in any manner whatsoever without written permission.

Without limiting the author's and publisher's exclusive rights, any unauthorized use of this publication to train generative artificial intelligence (AI) technologies is expressly prohibited.

This is a work of fiction. Names, characters, places and incidents are either the product of the author's imagination or are used fictitiously. Any resemblance to actual persons, living or dead, businesses, companies, events or locales is entirely coincidental.

For questions and comments about the quality of this book, please contact us at CustomerService@Harlequin.com.

TM and ® are trademarks of Harlequin Enterprises ULC.

Harlequin Enterprises ULC
22 Adelaide St. West, 41st Floor
Toronto, Ontario M5H 4E3, Canada
www.Harlequin.com

HarperCollins Publishers
Macken House, 39/40 Mayor Street Upper,
Dublin 1, D01 C9W8, Ireland
www.HarperCollins.com

Printed in Lithuania

Multi-award-winning author **Leslie Marshman** writes novels featuring strong heroines, the heroes who love them and the bad guys who fear them. She called Denver home until she married a Texan without reading the fine print. Now she lives halfway between Houston and Galveston and embraces the humidity. When Leslie's not writing, you might find her camping at a lake, fishing pole in one hand and a book in the other. Visit her at lesliemarshman.com, Facebook.com/lesliemarshmanauthor, Instagram.com/leslie_marshman or @lesliemarshman on X.

Books by Leslie Marshman

Harlequin Intrigue

The Protectors of Boone County, Texas

Resolute Justice
Resolute Aim
Resolute Investigation
Resolute Bodyguard
Resolute Security

Scent Detection

Visit the Author Profile page at Harlequin.com.

CAST OF CHARACTERS

***Matt Franklin*—**A bodyguard who had been partners in a security company in California. When his partner moved home to Resolute, Texas, and started a new company, Matt joined him with the intention of buying in as a partner again.

***Erin Montgomery*—**The daughter of one of Boone County's wealthiest couples, Erin lives on her family's ranch, training and working with injured dressage horses at the behest of her mother. But that's not her life's dream.

***Hank Caldwell*—**An aging ranch hand who's worked for the Montgomerys for decades. Now Hank just helps Erin with *her* horses. He has become her best friend and confidant.

***Alex Townsend*—**Erin's ex-boyfriend Alex involved her in a robbery ten years ago. Now he's out of prison and threatening to harm everyone she cares about if she doesn't help him find the missing loot.

***Nate Reed*—**A security expert who had half owned one of the most successful companies in California, Nate moved back to his Texas hometown after falling in love. He and Matt sold their SoCal company, and now Nate owns Resolute Security.

Chapter One

Boone County, Texas
The Montgomery Ranch

"Walk," Erin Montgomery commanded in the soft, firm voice she used with all her animals. She took a step forward and the jet-black horse fell in behind her, kicking up dust as they rounded the corral for another lap. Trained to perform specialized movements at the direction of his rider, Redemption had been limping since his last dressage competition. After the vet diagnosed ligament inflammation, the valuable Dutch Warmblood horse had come to the Montgomery Ranch for physical therapy.

"Halt."

Redemption stopped, shaking his head and snorting. Erin leaned forward until her forehead rested against the gelding's neck, stroking him with a gloved hand. "Yes, I feel it too, boy." It was an uneasiness that came from more than just the stiff wind that suddenly kicked up, cutting like a blade of ice. Dry leaves and dirt took to the air as the sky darkened to a slate gray.

Erin turned up the collar on her thick barn jacket, then reached around her neck for her bandanna, pulling it up over her nose and mouth. "Might be one of those winters when we get some snow, boy." But it wasn't the weather making her as skittish as the gelding.

Choices she'd made ten years ago were reaching out from the past like poison tendrils of acid rain. Burning into her soul, her confidence, even her ability to discern good from evil, right from wrong. She'd made so many poor decisions that she no longer trusted herself, and that insecurity had led to her current purgatory—stuck on her parents' dressage training ranch. It wasn't that she didn't love horses, but dressage was not where her heart lay.

You don't deserve your heart's content.

And she didn't. Not after everything she'd done, and no amount of penance would ever wipe that slate clean.

Redemption lifted his head with a jerk, nostrils flaring. Erin tightened her grip on the training rope as the prized animal pulled back from her.

"Settle down, boy," she cooed. But when he refused to be calmed, she yanked her bandanna down in case it was spooking him. "Easy, boy, e—" Another icy gust blew dirt into her mouth and whipped away her words.

She and Redemption danced in an awkward circle until Erin finally saw the reason for the horse's distress. A man, leaning his forearms against the top rail on the far side of the corral, was staring them down.

Erin squinted against the swirling dust, trying to figure out who he was. He wore a heavy jacket, with the hood from a sweatshirt underneath pulled over his head. Between that and his dark beard, mustache and sunglasses, not much of his face was visible.

Redemption pawed the ground, and Erin refocused on the horse. She calmed him down enough to tie his lead rope to the nearest fence post before striding toward the stranger, one hand curled around the pepper spray in her jacket pocket. Erin wasn't normally so jittery, but ever since—

From the corner of her eye, she saw her family's longtime ranch hand, Hank Caldwell, standing in the open doorway of the barn. He was nearing seventy but was still strong enough to take down a stubborn calf that didn't want to be branded. And Hank always wore his gun.

"I don't know who you are, but you're trespassing. And I'm sure you know that, considering all the signs posted along the fence lines." Inside her other jacket pocket, her fingers rested on her phone. "And that you need a security code to open the gate."

The man didn't move. Didn't smile. Didn't speak. His silent stare spooked her far more than if he'd made an aggressive move.

"Fine. Have it your way." Erin pulled her phone out. "I'm calling the police."

"Ah, come on, *Eriss*. Is that any way to treat an old friend?"

She froze at the sound of his voice. A voice she hadn't heard in years. The deep Texas twang he'd acquired and then kept to convince others he was born here.

He'd convinced a lot of people.

Including her.

But what really sent a shiver down her spine was hearing the nickname Alex Townsend had given her after the first time they kissed. An endearment that combined Erin and heiress, a shared intimacy that had once made her smile but now turned her stomach.

Calling on years of hiding her true emotions to keep

the shock and fear from her face, Erin forced a hard edge to her tone. "I heard you finally made parole."

"Yeah. Finally." His mouth twisted into a smirk. "For some strange reason, time off for good behavior eluded me." He pushed his hood back, revealing scars on his forehead and closely shaved scalp.

Erin studied his face, at once familiar to her and yet changed in a way that defied definition. Older, obviously. Harder, maybe. His once straight nose now bent to the right, the center of it a mass of scar tissue. A jagged line crossed up one cheek and continued through his brow, just missing his eye. Souvenirs from his time in prison, apparently.

She made a show of looking toward Hank. "I suggest you leave now."

Alex flashed her the smile that used to make her insides flutter, that charmed her into believing every word he said. That even convinced her to take part in a crime. "Come on, Erin. I'm just here to talk. I've missed you. Thought you would have visited me once in a while, or at least accepted a collect call or two."

Funny how that smile did nothing to her now. "Leave or I'm calling the police. Your choice."

"Whoa, baby. Relax. If you don't want to get back together, fine." He gave her an exaggerated shrug. "Just give me my half of the haul plus interest, and I'll be on my way."

Still trying to get past the *get back together* comment, it took Erin several seconds for the rest of what he said to sink in. "Interest? Half of the haul? What on earth are you talking about?"

Alex glanced over at Hank, then leaned closer to Erin.

"You're the only one who could have taken everything we stole. I just want my fair share, plus a bit more for my pain and suffering. Ten years behind bars and this—" he pointed to his damaged face "—are worth the extra."

Erin frowned. "You're crazy." She regretted the phrase the moment the words left her mouth, remembering how it affected him. He'd donned an almost flawless persona during his con years. Being everyone's friend, convincing the special few he'd chosen at the charity where they'd met that his ideas were actually theirs. But even a joke about Alex or his ideas being crazy brought out the darkness in him. A darkness Erin eventually learned was his true self.

His hands shot over the top rail and grabbed her jacket collar on either side, yanking her hard against the fence. "I've waited a long time for this, Erin. And your innocent act ain't working. Everything we stole that night didn't just up and disappear into thin air. The cops never found it, not even after you turned traitor and told them where it was."

Alex jerked her harder, and Erin dropped her phone and braced her hands against the fence to keep from having her face smashed into his. She tried to pull away, but his strength was too much. He leaned even closer, his face almost touching hers, his eyes burning with malice. Having the fence as a barrier between them should have afforded Erin a modicum of safety, but it didn't.

His breath hot and foul on her face, Alex continued. "Three of us went to prison and Jensen ran. You're the only one who could've taken it."

Erin's mouth went as dry as the West Texas plains, and her heartbeat kicked into double time. "Jensen must have taken it, then. Because I don't have it."

"I already tracked him down. He died a month after he left here, shot while holding up a convenience store in San Antonio and buried in a pauper's grave. Trust me, he didn't take the jewelry."

"All you have to do is read the police reports." Erin spoke with the soft but firm voice she used with her horses. All the while, she pulled against his grip. "I was still sitting in the police station when the cops went to retrieve the bag. I couldn't have moved it."

Alex scoffed. "Not my problem, sweetheart."

Hank, by now standing behind Alex, leveled his gun at him with a steady hand. "Get your hands off her, or I'll drop you where you stand."

"Take it easy. We're just having a little reunion." Alex released her, his hands up in mock surrender.

"I suggest you reunion yourself off this property." Hank moved a step closer.

"On my way." Alex turned his glare back on Erin. "If you don't already have it, you best get to treasure hunting, and fast. I got to you once. I can get to you again, and no old man is going to stop me. You've got until the end of the month. Once I get my share—and don't forget the interest—you'll never hear from me again."

"That's just two weeks away."

"Yep. You better get busy."

"You're wasting your time, Alex. Trust me, I have nothing to give you and no idea where the jewelry could be. Now get out of here before I have Hank shoot you."

"Trust you? Traitors don't inspire trust, sweetheart. I suggest you rethink your answer. Because one thing I've learned is, you don't get people to do things for you by threatening them. You get people to do things by threatening the people they love." Alex looked at Hank. "Better sleep with one eye open, old man."

"I sleep with my gun in my hand, cocked and ready, you punk. Now git!"

Alex looked back at Erin, his smile lazy and cruel. "Give my regards to Ma and Pa Montgomery." And with that, he turned and sauntered away.

Hank came up to her. "You okay, Erin?"

"A bit shaken, but fine."

"I'll let all the ranch hands know to watch out for him. We won't let that son of a— We won't let him back on the property."

"Thanks, Hank."

"Nothing to thank me for."

Hank left her there, staring after Alex's retreating form long after he'd disappeared, the cold seeping into her bones having nothing to do with the weather.

MATT FRANKLIN PUSHED through the front door of Resolute Security, humming an old '60s tune still popular with surfers. What he wouldn't give to paddle out into the surf and catch a good wave. When he'd joined Nate in Texas, he lamented leaving the West Coast behind. Nate had mentioned how close Resolute was to Matagorda Bay, but the warm, murky waters of the Gulf were a far cry from the blue chill of the Pacific Ocean, especially when it came to surfing.

Still, working with Nate was worth the sacrifice. Becoming a partner in Resolute Security was worth even more.

"Hey, boss man." Matt dropped into the chair facing the reception desk. "You've got a job for me?"

The storefront office had three rooms: Nate's office, a space to meet with clients and the small reception area. Its location next door to a private investigator's office was perfect, especially since the PI was Nate's brother-in-law Trevor Bishop, and referrals between the two businesses helped both companies grow.

"Yes, and it's a well-paying one." Nate opened a file folder and glanced at the paperwork inside. "Jim and Holly Montgomery live on an eight-hundred-acre ranch up in Winston. They're part of what you'd call Boone County's elite. Jim's an international venture capitalist. Holly, aside from being a prominent socialite, runs a dressage training and rehab business."

"Boone County has an elite? And socialites?" Matt chuckled. "I must have missed that in the orientation meeting."

Nate looked up, smiling. "I'll grant you that Boone County doesn't compare to the glamour of Hollywood, but the Montgomerys are heavy hitters in the political arena and are always on the A-list for charity galas, stuff like that." Nate leaned back in his chair. "Holly called first thing this morning, requesting a bodyguard."

"So, what's the job?"

"Mr. and Mrs. are overseas on one of Jim's business trips, and their daughter Erin's home alone. She needs round-the-clock protection."

Matt groaned at the thought of babysitting some rich kid. "Don't they have staff to take care of their children?"

The smile—no, smirk—taking over Nate's face made Matt cringe. He'd seen that look before, always followed by a punch line. "Erin is twenty-eight."

Matt raised a brow. "Okay, you got me. But you still haven't explained why she needs protection."

Nate's grin vanished. "She had a threatening visit from Alex Townsend, thirty-four, an ex-boyfriend who thinks he has a pretty big ax to grind. Her parents are convinced he poses a real danger and have hired us to keep her safe." He slid the file across the desk. "Long story short, Erin got into trouble when she was a teen. Part of a group that robbed the guests at her parents' charity gala."

"Wait. If her family's so wealthy, why..." Matt shook his head as his words trailed off.

"She was in love." Nate shrugged. "Anyway, they caught her, but she cooperated with the police by turning in her boyfriend and the other three men involved. Also told the police where the gang hid the stash, although it was never recovered. There's still a reward for anyone who turns it in. Because of her confession, her age and her parents' influence with the previous county judge, she was released on probation."

Matt flipped pages in the file. "What about the other three? Are they bothering her, too?"

"Brad Parker and Kevin Moore are still in prison. Billy Jensen died during another robbery ten years ago. But now Townsend, the leader of the gang, is out and harassing the daughter. Says he wants his half of the loot, which Erin claims not to have."

"You believe her?"

"It doesn't matter whether I do or not. What matters is—"

"Keeping the client safe." Matt rested one ankle on the opposite knee. "Is ten years the usual term for robbery in Texas?"

"*Armed* robbery and aggravated assault."

"And yet the girl walked away with no jail time?" Matt blew out a breath. "Unbelievable."

"She wasn't armed, she was young and she cooperated with the police." Nate gave Matt a pointed look. "So yes, she got a second chance."

"Bottom line, she wasn't held accountable for her actions."

"Bottom line, she's in danger and we've taken the job of protecting her." Nate leaned forward, resting his forearms on the desk blotter. "This is a high-paying job from people who could refer other wealthy clients to us. And we need the money."

"You know how I feel about second chances."

A moment of silence hung in the air between them. "I get it, Matt. If your mom hadn't given your dad a second chance, she'd still be alive. But you and I have protected plenty of people we wouldn't want to be friends with. And this job is nothing like what happened with your parents." Nate drummed his fingers on his desk. "It could bring in a good chunk of what you need to buy your half of the company. That's why I want *you* to take it."

Matt's goal was to become a fifty-fifty partner with Nate, just as they'd been in California. When they'd sold Reed and Franklin Security in Los Angeles and Nate returned to Texas, Matt made the mistake of staying in the Golden State for what he thought was a combo job/romance gig, emphasis on the romance. Boy, had he called that one wrong. Although he'd invested what he had left when he arrived in Resolute, he still needed to chip in more to become an equal partner. A lot more.

He shrugged. "A job's a job." Matt stood, holding up the folder. "This my copy?"

"It is." Nate paused, then added, "I'm sure I don't need to remind you of this, but…"

"I know, I know—"

In unison, they both said, "Don't fall in love with the client."

"I promise you, boss man, there's not a snowball's chance in Texas of that happening."

After his fiasco in California with Meryl Duncan, agent to the stars, Matt was on the wagon where women were concerned. Not that he had much to worry about with this case. He knew from firsthand experience that giving someone a second chance was for chumps, and he was no chump.

Chapter Two

After swinging by his shabby but affordable apartment to throw some clothes in his duffel bag, Matt headed northwest toward Winston, Texas. Although Resolute was the county seat, Winston, according to Nate, was bigger and had its own police force.

Thirty minutes later, a low whistle escaped his lips as he drove along the fence line of the Montgomery Ranch. When he reached the locked entrance gate, he stopped and stared. This place might be called a ranch, but instead of a large rustic house made of logs and beams, Matt gaped at what looked like a contemporary mansion plopped down in the middle of Texas.

Pressing the buzzer for the gate several times brought no response, so Matt tapped in the code Nate had gotten from Mrs. Montgomery. A barn and another building sat a good way off to the left and behind the house. A note in the file from Nate directed him to go past the big house and find his client at the barn or the bunkhouse near it. He followed the interior paved road to the house, where it made a circle drive around a life-size bronze statue of a horse, its mane in weird little knots.

A gravel road split off to the right and curved around the back of the house. Matt followed it to the barn, parked next to a shiny red pickup and turned the key in his ignition to Off.

As the cooling engine pinged, he sucked in a breath and exhaled slowly. Time to put on his poker face. A good bodyguard never reflected their true feelings about a client, especially if those feelings were negative.

He stepped from his truck. A chilly day for sure, but his heater worked like a champ, keeping him toasty. He left his jacket and duffel bag in the vehicle for now while he got the lay of the land.

As Matt walked toward the buildings, he checked out the property, assessing avenues of potential threats and means for protection. So much open space was both a good and bad thing. Easy to spot incoming threats while at the same time hard to cover all potential places of ingress.

He'd have his work cut out for him.

He reached the closed-up barn, surprised to see another security code lock on the doors. With no one in the nearby corral, he headed to the log cabin. It was farther from the barn than it had looked from a distance, sitting on higher ground.

Another door bearing a security code lock. After knocking and getting no response, he peered through the windows, seeing no signs of life. His client could be off running errands. Or she could be lying inside, dead at the hands of her ex-boyfriend.

Matt tried the front gate code on the door and it opened. He took in the log walls, rustic wood ceiling with beams and a small kitchen off to one side. Three doors led to rooms partitioned off along the back wall of the building, and he peered into each one. A bedroom with a freestanding wardrobe, dresser and a bed. A small bathroom. And behind door number three, what looked to be a combination junk/storage room, jammed with boxes and bins, a full garment rack and more pairs of Western boots than a shoe store.

But no Erin Montgomery.

He jogged back to the barn and punched in the same code there. When he swung the door open, the view inside the barn grabbed his attention.

A woman, presumably Erin Montgomery, stood in the middle of the barn with her back toward Matt, brushing a horse as gold as a ray of sun. She wore a heavy jacket, jeans and cowboy boots, and her long dark hair hung in braids, swinging with each sweep of the brush across the horse's flank.

"Hello," Matt said, still at the barn's entrance.

Nothing.

He tried again, louder. "Hello!"

Still no response.

Matt walked up behind her and tapped her shoulder. The woman jumped, and the brush flew out of her hand, straight up in the air and down. Right on top of his head. Swearing under his breath, he reached up and rubbed the spot where a lump was already forming.

The woman spun toward him. Matt had only a second to confirm her face matched the picture in the file before Erin's hand disappeared into her jacket pocket and reappeared, holding a small cylinder in her fist.

"No, no—" was all he got out before she shoved her hand toward his face and pepper-sprayed him. "Son of a—" Ducking his head, Matt yelled, "Stop! I'm Matt Franklin, your bodyguard!" His face burned, his mouth burned, his eyes burned most of all. Tears streamed down his face and he coughed as he stumbled blindly back toward the door and outside.

"I don't have a bodyguard!" Erin yelled back at him as if she thought blinding him also rendered him deaf. "I'm calling the police!"

"Go ahead. I'll have them arrest you for assault." Man, his eyes were on fire. He could not get them to stay open.

"And I'll have them arrest you for trespassing."

"Fine, but could you get me some water while we wait?" Matt wheezed before dissolving into another coughing fit.

"Why should I?"

He used his shirttail to wipe his watering eyes, but it did nothing to ease the pain. "Look, lady, I'm here by invitation. How 'bout you cut me some slack?"

After a moment, Erin yelled, "Stand still!"

A wall of water hit him full on in the face, drenching his whole upper body. "Are you kidding me?" He tried to squint, but his eyes remained closed. He yanked apart the snaps on his shirt and dropped the wet garment on the ground in case another dousing was coming.

The cold air latched on to his wet skin and drew out goose bumps by the score.

"Here." Erin grabbed his hand and yanked him forward a few steps. "If you don't like the way I do it, you can do it yourself. The water's right in front of you."

Matt groped until his hands made out the edge of a metal pail of water. He wrapped one arm around its middle and hoisted it to his chest. Cupping his free hand, he splashed water on his face over and over.

"Listen, buster, you've got one minute to explain yourself before I call the police."

Matt's eyes still burned, but he was no longer having coughing spasms. His temper, however, hung by a thread that was getting thinner by the moment. "No, you listen, Princess. Your parents hired a bodyguard from Resolute Security. I'm that bodyguard." Matt kept splashing water on his face as he spoke. "And why are you yelling?"

"Oh. I forgot I had my earbuds in."

She must've removed them, because Matt could hear the song playing even from where he stood. He stopped splashing water on his face and turned his head to where he guessed she might be. "And the music wasn't a clue?"

"Hey. You're the intruder here. No one hired a bodyguard for me, and when I prove it, I'm having you arrested."

"Bring it on."

ERIN FISHED HER phone out of her pocket. The only thing that could make things worse right now would be confronting her mother, so she called her father.

"Erin? Is everything all right?" Her dad's concerned voice boomed in her ear.

"I'm fine, Dad. Listen, I'm putting you on speaker." *Let this jerk hear Dad's denial himself.* "There's a guy here who says he's my bodyguard. I say he's a liar. You didn't hire a bodyguard for me, did you?"

The beat of silence that followed chipped away at her certainty.

"Ah, that's your mother's doing."

Of course.

"She heard you were having trouble with that guy from before and wanted to make sure you're safe."

Guy from before. The closest anyone in the family ever got to mentioning Alex's name. Or the robbery.

"I'm sure she meant to call you about it."

"Well, she didn't, and I nearly killed the man when he showed up here." Erin turned away from Matt and spoke through gritted teeth. "Dad, you need to talk to Mom. Tell her I don't want this bodyguard. Any bodyguard. Hank is here. He'll watch out for me."

"Sweetie, you know how your mother gets when she sets her mind to something. It's easier to just accept it."

"Yeah, Dad, I know." Erin sighed. "I just wish you would…" *stand up to her.* She couldn't bring herself to finish the sentence aloud. She may not respect her father for always giving in to her mother, but she'd never tell him that to his face.

"Sorry, Erin, you caught me just as I was walking into a meeting." And just like that—just like always—her father was back to his upbeat, path-of-least-resistance self. "I've got to go. Love you."

Erin closed her eyes and took a deep breath. "Love you, too, Dad." Her anger toward Matt for scaring her faded, but the anger at being handled by her overbearing mother still simmered under the surface. Resigning herself to her fate, as well as an apology she needed to make, she turned back to her injured bodyguard.

"I guess I owe you an apology." She cringed at the sight of his red and swollen eyes. "My mother didn't bother to fill me in on her little plan." Then, trying to regain a modicum of dignity, she added, "But you shouldn't have snuck up on me. If you'd buzzed from the gate, we could have resolved this without the pepper spray."

"I might be more inclined to accept that apology when I can open my eyes without pain." Matt wheezed and coughed some more. "And I did buzz. No one answered. Maybe because, *earbuds*?"

She ignored the dig. "So, how *did* you get in?"

"Your parents gave us the security code for the gate."

Alex's visit had scared her plenty, but the last thing she wanted was some stranger underfoot. Hank would have everyone on alert, and she was half tempted to arm herself full-time.

"Look, I don't need a bodyguard. Our ranch hands are aware of the situation, and they're armed. So, if you need me to call your boss to cancel this, I will."

"First, that's not how this works. Only the person who hires us can cancel the job. Second, is pepper-spraying people something you do on the regular?" Matt put a thumb below his right eye and a forefinger on the upper lid and tried to pry it open. "Because it's not usually a thing someone does who's not afraid for their life."

The remark stoked her anger, but mostly because he was right. She'd started carrying the pepper spray after the robbery. After she'd seen Alex's dark side the first time. Erin grabbed the empty bucket from him and refilled it. "Here." She shoved the pail against his chest. "I'm going to finish brushing my horse."

"Don't wander off when you're done."

"Or what?" she threw back over her shoulder. Blind as he was, he'd be hard-pressed to stop her. And she needed to be away from him, away from every controlling person in her life. Space. That's what she needed. And the comfort she got from the horses she cared for.

Fear gnawed at her, but even more overwhelming was the exhaustion and frustration of having no control over her own life.

HALF AN HOUR LATER, her horse was back in its stall, and Erin had calmed herself enough to check on Matt. It would be a whole lot easier to stay irritated with his presence if he'd left his shirt on. Although not bulked up like a bodybuilder, his six-pack rippled with each splash of water to his face and, well, she was used to judging fine horseflesh. Not much difference in judging a fine male form; nothing more than an analytical, objective perusal.

"Are your eyes feeling better?" She picked up the pail at his feet and refilled it again.

His red-rimmed eyes squinted at the water she scooped up. "You've been giving me water from a horse trough to rinse my face?"

Erin almost laughed out loud. "That's a rain barrel, not a horse trough. It's clean water." Erin shook her head. "You aren't from around here, are you?"

Matt picked up his shirt and shook it out. "California. But even if I *was* from Texas, I wouldn't be living on a ranch with—" he waved his hands in the air "—horses and troughs and…and stuff like that."

"A city boy, then. And here I thought you must be a genuine cowboy, what with that pearl snap shirt and all." Erin smiled as her gaze drifted from Matt's broad chest down to his chiseled abs and narrow waist. Analytical and objective. Nothing more. "I bet you'd make a good one."

"Trust me, I'm about as far from cowboy as you can

get. And the shirt was a gift." He pulled the damp garment on but left it hanging open. "Now, how 'bout you show me where we're sleeping?"

Where *we're* sleeping?

Forget that. If it was the last thing she did, she was getting rid of Matt Franklin and his shirtless abs. He'd see. Her mother would see. Alex Townsend would see. It was all a part of her grand plan to take control of her life.

MATT PICKED UP his duffel bag and jacket that he'd retrieved from his vehicle while Erin finished grooming her horse.

"Where we're sleeping?" Erin repeated in a tone reminiscent of his third-grade parochial teacher. The one who'd smacked his knuckles with a ruler more than once. "*I* sleep in the bunkhouse. I have no idea where *you'll* be sleeping." She glanced at his old, beat-up truck parked next to hers. "Don't you stay in your truck for stakeouts?"

"This isn't a stakeout. I'm providing round-the-clock protection. Which means I go where you go, and I live where you live."

"That's not going to work for me." She tipped her head toward the small log cabin bunkhouse. "There's barely enough room in there for me. And I value my privacy."

"I like my privacy, too, but this isn't forever. We'll figure it out." Getting new clients familiar with protection protocols was always a process. Matt found it best to just rip off the Band-Aid. He started across the shallow incline toward his soon-to-be temporary home. "Best place to start is with sleeping arrangements."

Quick footsteps pounded behind him. "Wait a minute. You can't barge into someone's home uninvited."

Matt turned to face her while walking backward. "I already have. Technically your parents own the bunkhouse, and your mother invited me here." He tried not to laugh as she raced ahead to reach the front door first.

"What do you mean, you already have?" She spoke through clenched teeth while blocking his entrance.

"Relax." He stepped onto the porch. "I couldn't find you, and I needed to make sure you weren't hurt. Or, you know, dead."

Erin's eyes narrowed. "My parents are away, so there's no reason you can't stay in the main house. You'll have the place to yourself, and you can see the bunkhouse from there."

Her response confirmed that he'd accomplished step one: getting the client to accept that a bodyguard was a part of their life. Now Erin needed to accept that he, the bodyguard, set the rules.

"When a bodyguard guards a body, both the bodyguard and the body need to be near each other at all times." Matt reached past her, turned the handle and pushed the door open. "After you."

From the set of her jaw, she had no intention of moving. Time for a little truth strategy.

"Look, I'm not here to ruin your life," he said. "I'm here to do a job. And you… Well, I read the file on Alex Townsend. He was a nasty piece of work before he went to prison, and trust me, he didn't improve any while serving time. He spent more time in solitary confinement because of fighting than he did in gen pop." When she raised a questioning brow, he clarified, "General population."

She gave a nod as if she'd known that.

"The owner of Resolute Security is the brother of

Boone County Sheriff Cassie Reed. She's aware that Townsend is back in town and that he threatened you. Winston Police Chief Simpson knows as well. It seems he filed your restraining order request with the judge, but they haven't been able to serve it yet because Townsend keeps disappearing."

"Of course he does," Erin muttered.

"Unfortunately, even if he had been served, there's no proof Alex trespassed or violated it."

"Hank was here. He can testify."

"It's still 'he said, she said.' And by the time he's found and hauled to court, it could be too late for you." He softened his tone even more. "Your parents think he poses enough of a threat that they hired me. And you carry pepper spray, so you must be worried. How about, just for now, we figure out a way to make this work?"

She hesitated, then said with an imperious lift of her chin, "For your information, I always carry pepper spray." She arched a brow, reminding him she wasn't afraid to use it. Then she spun around and clomped across the hardwood floor, holding out her arms. "This is it. Home sweet home."

Step two, check.

Having already been inside the cabin, Matt crossed the threshold and began a mental list of security needs. Locking pins for one, two…four, five, six windows. Motion detectors, too. The front door had a keypad dead bolt lock, but he wanted to add a manual dead bolt only operable from the inside. Lighting needed to be added around the perimeter, and the shrubs under the windows needed to be clipped back.

"Like I said, I didn't expect anyone to stay here. But

if you're determined to, that's the only spare room." She twisted her mouth to the side as she pointed to the junk room. "Sorry."

Oh, she wasn't sorry at all, but Matt refused to give her the satisfaction. "No problem. I can sleep on the couch." He crossed the room and sat, sinking into the oversize piece of furniture. "Ah, this will be just fine."

"You can't sleep there. That's where I relax in the evenings. You'd be in my way."

"I won't stretch out with my pillow until after you go to bed."

"Nope." Erin shook her head. "You on the couch just won't work for me."

Matt arched a brow at her when she offered no solution to his lack of sleeping accommodations.

"Well, make yourself at home. I have an appointment in town this afternoon and need to shower off the barn dust and horse dander." Erin didn't exactly slam the bathroom door but closed it with…emphasis. Then locked it.

Matt chuckled. She was a spitfire.

As soon as the water came on, he headed into the junk room. He stood with his hands on his hips for a moment, surveying the mess, then got to work.

He was back on the couch by the time Erin appeared in clean clothes. She'd been cute in the barn with braids, but cute gave way to pretty with her long, dark hair hanging loose and framing her face. Not that he was interested in second-chance socialites.

"As long as we're heading to town, I need to pick up an air bed."

"An air bed?" She made a point of surveying the couch,

coffee table and TV that took up most of the small living area.

"Not for out here." Matt stood and walked toward the extra room. "But there's plenty of space in here."

"You must be out of your—" She stopped at the doorway.

He'd moved the boxes and storage bins until they lined two walls, stacked three high. The garment rack, holding an assortment of long-sleeved shirts, Henleys, tank tops and T-shirts, with folded jeans on the bottom shelf, sat against the wall with the door. And he'd arranged her many pairs of boots in two rows along the fourth wall.

"See? Plenty of room for an air bed." Matt held his breath. People seldom appreciated uninvited guests moving things around.

Erin chuckled, her reaction surprising him. "Wow. I hope you don't charge extra for housework." When she smiled, all her hard edges softened.

"First time's free. Part of our introductory offer." He winked, then followed her into the room. "I'm curious. What's with all the boxes? Is that where you store your ball gowns and diamond tiaras?"

She'd been facing away from him, but at his question, Erin turned back, her smile gone. She walked past him and out the front door.

Matt hadn't seen anyone's demeanor change that fast since his ex-girlfriend changed her locks. Something had set Erin off, putting him back to square one with her. Just when things had been going so well.

He joined her outside, sitting beside her on the porch swing. "I'm sorry if I said anything to offend you."

"No reason to apologize. It just reminded me of something unpleasant from a long time ago." Erin stared off across the property. "You better get a move on if you want to get that bed before the stores close."

With the sun high above them, Matt looked at his watch. "It's not even noon."

"It's a small town. You might have trouble finding one."

"Then get your shoes on and let's go." Matt stood, but Erin stayed put.

"That's okay. I've got some things to do around here while you're gone." She finally looked at him, her face showing no anger, no emotion at all.

"You said you have an appointment in town."

"I can reschedule it. You run along, and I'll see you when you get back."

Oops. Apparently step two needed a refresher course. "That's not the way this—" he pointed back and forth between the two of them "—relationship works. The bodyguarding has begun. I won't be going anywhere without you, and you won't be going anywhere without me."

"In other words, if I don't go, you don't have anywhere to sleep." She folded her arms across her chest. "That's a shame, but not my problem, Mr. *Bodyguard*."

Matt hid a smile. So, she wanted to play hardball, eh? Fine by him. He may not be a cowboy, but this wasn't his first rodeo. "It will be your problem, because I plan to sleep in a bed tonight, and right now the only available one in this bunkhouse is yours." Matt mirrored her folded arms and stubborn glare. "So unless you want to sleep on the couch, I suggest *you* get a move on."

Chapter Three

Erin stewed as she stared through the windshield during the quiet ride into town. For someone determined to take charge of her life, she seemed to have less control by the second. Her mother's infernal interference, her dad's apathy. A bodyguard in her life, in her home, in her business. And he came with a passel of *don't-do-this* rules. Alex back, threatening her and those she loved, demanding jewels she didn't have.

She felt like a passive participant in her own existence. And she hated that feeling.

Though unfair, Matt proved a convenient target for her frustration. True, he was part of the problem. True, she still planned on getting rid of him, the sooner the better. And yet, it was unfair to take it all out on him. Even so, she was giving him the silent treatment. And all because of his crack about gowns and tiaras. How mature was that? No way he could know how close he'd come to Alex's past comments about her family's wealth. It had been how Alex preyed upon her, capitalizing on her feelings of privileged guilt.

Erin broke the silence when they passed a speed-limit sign. "Don't go over the limit by even one mile. The Winston cops are famous for their monthly ticket quotas."

Matt eased his foot off the gas, coasting as they approached the first buildings. "Any idea where we should try first?"

"The hardware store should have the air bed." She didn't mention it was also where she'd planned to go today, but by herself. "Take a right at the stop sign. It's down about a block."

"Okay. After that, I need to swing by the grocery store, pick up a few things."

"I've got a fully stocked kitchen."

"Yeah, I checked it out while you were in the shower." Matt pulled into a parking space in front of Hudson's Hardware. "But there are some things I like that you don't have."

By the time Matt killed the engine, Erin had unfastened her shoulder harness and had her hand on the door handle.

"Not so fast." He pushed the door-lock button. "We went over this. Wait until I get around to your side, then unlock the door."

"Seriously?"

"I'm dead serious. If someone wants to hurt you, they could get at you as soon as you step out of the truck."

"Trust me, Alex isn't going to hurt me unless I—" Erin snapped her mouth shut and turned her face away.

"Unless you what?"

Unless I don't find the jewelry.

"Unless I'm isolated," she improvised. "You really think he's stupid enough to come after me in a town full of people?"

"I have no idea how stupid he is, just as I'm pretty sure

you're not telling me everything I need to know about this whole situation."

Was she that obvious?

He climbed out, rounded the front of the truck and unlocked her door with his key fob.

"This seems like overkill." Erin climbed out into what amounted to a wide, loose embrace from Matt.

"Just pretend I'm being a gentleman."

She looked up into his eyes. "*Are* you a gentleman?"

Matt's only answer was his sly smile, combined with the twinkle in those impenetrable blue eyes.

They entered the store, and Erin was glad to be out of the cold. But Matt was stuck to her side like they'd been superglued together. She needed an alternate plan to buy her supplies without him being aware.

While Matt shopped for an air bed that suited his apparent Princess-and-the-Pea syndrome, she pulled a scrap of paper and a pen from her purse. At the checkout, Erin insisted on paying for the mattress, and passed her note to Betty, the cashier, with her credit card.

The note had her shopping list and a request to deliver the items to the main house. Mission accomplished.

Twenty minutes later, they'd worked their way through almost every aisle of the grocery store except produce and health foods.

"You do know that most of this stuff will kill you, right?" Erin rummaged through the cart filled with what she considered stress-eating foods: packages of cookies and crackers, bags of chips and candy, protein bars of questionable nutritional value.

Matt tossed a bag of kettle corn into the cart. "Sometimes you have to weigh the balance between physical and mental health. And based on today, which is barely half over, I'm more concerned with my sanity than my glucose or cholesterol levels."

"Are you implying that I—"

"I'm *implying* nothing." One corner of his mouth kicked up in a half smile, bringing out a small dimple.

Obviously, she was the reason for his stress eating. "You can always quit, you know."

"Nice try."

"Hi, Miss Erin."

They both turned toward the youthful voice behind them.

"Tommy! How are you?" Erin approached the nine-year-old boy and crouched to give him a hug.

"Who's that?" Tommy pointed at Matt, then whispered, "Is he your boyfriend?"

Laughing, Erin stood. "No, no, no. This is my friend Matt. Matt, this is Tommy Barrows. I give him riding lessons."

"Nice to meet you, Tommy." Matt stepped closer to the boy. "You like horses, huh?"

Tommy tilted his head back and looked up at Matt. "Yep. Miss Erin says I'll get to ride outside of the corral pretty soon."

"Dude!" Matt held his hand out for a high five. "*I* can't even ride outside the corral."

Tommy smacked his hand, a smile overtaking his face. "Wanna see what I found?"

"Sure." Matt crouched next to him while Tommy dug in his jeans pocket.

Just then, Tommy's mother rounded the corner, pushing a cart. "Tommy! I've been looking everywhere for you."

"Hi, Jill." Erin joined her friend near the end of the aisle. "He's okay. Just showing my…friend his latest find."

Jill gave her a questioning look that said she wanted to know more about Erin's friend but kept the conversation on Tommy. "I swear, that boy and his gewgaws. He found a big, old marble, what we called shooters in my day." Jill chuckled. "He thinks the twists in the center look like an eye."

Erin's gaze drifted down the aisle to the boy and the man. Tommy, his arms and hands moving as he spoke, and Matt nodding, smiling and widening his eyes as if in awe. No way a grown man could be that astonished by an old marble. But Matt acted as though it was the most amazing thing he'd ever seen.

Jill stepped closer and nudged Erin. "So, who's your friend?" she whispered. "Don't think I've seen him around before."

Erin wasn't about to share the ex-boyfriend/bodyguard story with anyone. "Not what you're thinking. He's just a friend, visiting for a week or so."

"Well, that's a shame, 'cause he's definitely got a new fan. He sure is good with kids."

"Yes, he is," Erin murmured. "Isn't he?"

"Don't be surprised if Tommy brings his whole triple S collection to his next lesson."

Erin cocked her head to the side. "Triple S?"

"Shiny, sparkly or strange." Jill laughed. "That pretty much describes everything that catches his eye."

"You've got that right," Erin agreed, smiling. But her

attention was still drawn to the attractive bodyguard who could make a little boy happy so quickly.

There was more to Matt Franklin than she'd assumed, and that troubled her for reasons she couldn't define.

"Where do I turn?" Matt had reluctantly agreed to stop at a long-term care facility on the way back to the Montgomerys' ranch so Erin could visit a friend. Reluctant, because this was yet another stop, after the liquor store, she hadn't informed him of when they set out. He'd been clear on travel protocols for leaving the ranch, but she wasn't complying. That didn't bode well for his ability to keep her safe. He needed to set her straight.

As she sorted her grocery purchases, transferring items from one bag to another, Erin said, "Turn left just past the giant live oak."

Matt glanced at her. "I might need a little more detail. There are a lot of oak trees out here."

Without looking up, Erin sighed. "Don't worry. You'll know it when you see it." She scraped at a price label on a jar of gourmet jam with her thumbnail.

"So, who are we going to visit?"

Erin lifted her head. "Liam O'Roarke. He's an old friend of my father's."

"You're visiting him because your dad's out of town and can't?"

"No." A shadow passed over her face. "I visit him every week."

Huh. Not something he'd expect a spoiled socialite to do.

The biggest oak tree he'd ever seen loomed ahead on

the left, and he slowed to take the turn. A sign announced the Hidden Oaks Care Facility. An apt name.

"This is the driveway. Keep straight, and it's just beyond the rise in the road."

Matt pulled into a parking space near the front door. "Not many visitors here, based on the empty parking lot."

"It's busier on weekends and holidays. A lot of people swing by after work." Erin opened the passenger door. "Some residents have spouses who still live in their own homes but can't drive, so they have to wait until someone can bring them. Luckily, Mrs. O'Roarke is younger than her husband and still going strong, so she comes by often."

Matt raised a brow at her, his eyes moving from her to the door and back. Shaking her head, Erin pulled the door closed and waited for him to come around and let her out.

"You know this is ridiculous, right? There's no one here."

"It's good practice, so it becomes a habit." Matt walked next to her toward the entrance.

"Good luck with that, Mr. Bodyguard. It takes six weeks to form a new habit." Erin scoffed. "And this—" she pointed back and forth between them "—is not going to be going on for six weeks."

"We can only hope." Matt followed her inside and waited while she signed them in, then they walked through a maze of hallways to a private room with an open door.

Erin crossed the room in a few long strides and set her bag down on the bed.

"How are you today, Liam?" She bent over, gently put her arms around his shoulders and gave him a long hug.

The smile on the old man's face was lopsided but big.

"Ah, grand, I am. And you, my girl?" Despite a shaky voice, his words carried across the room to Matt.

Erin straightened. "Pretty darn close to grand."

The old man's gaze drifted past Erin to Matt. "And who might this strapping young lad be? Don't tell me you finally took my advice and found yourself a gentleman friend."

Erin's face reddened, but to her credit, she recovered quickly. "You better quit your teasing, or I might stop sneaking contraband to you." They both laughed over the shared secret. "This is Matt Franklin. He's just a friend who I'm spending the day with."

"Well, the more the merrier, I always say." The old man smiled at Matt. "Pleased to meet you."

Matt stepped closer and offered his hand. "The pleasure's mine, sir."

The old man grimaced as he shook Matt's hand with his left one. "Oh, none of that *sir* stuff, now. I'm Liam." He sat in a wheelchair positioned close to his bed. Erin dropped onto the bed and motioned for Matt to take the recliner.

"Take care not to fall asleep in that thing, Matt." The old man chuckled. "When I sit there to watch TV, I can't even make it through a half-hour program."

"How's your shoulder feeling?" Erin set her hand on Liam's closest shoulder. "The other day you could barely move it."

"Much better. Between the ice, heat and massages, the old biddies have loosened it up."

Erin glanced at Matt. "He calls the nurses and aides here 'old biddies.'" She rolled her eyes. "Last week he got into a wheelchair race with one of his neighbors and overdid it."

"I was sure I could beat him, even with only one good arm. But I should have made him tie one hand behind his back. *Then* it would've been a fair race."

"And you'd likely be just as sore."

For the next hour, Matt watched as Erin asked Liam questions about his days, about what he'd been up to since her last visit, about his wife. She held the old man's left hand, and Matt noticed that Liam's right hand hadn't moved from his lap since they'd arrived.

She smoothed back a wisp of white hair falling over Liam's forehead, touched his arm with loving familiarity and leaned into him as they shared a laugh about something. Matt's opinion of her went up by a couple of notches, and he admitted, if only to himself, that there was more to the second-chance rich girl than he'd originally thought.

"I got you more of that fig jam you like. And look, your favorite cookies." As Erin pulled items out of the bag and showed off each one before setting them on his tray table, the old man's off-kilter grin grew bigger and bigger.

"You're going to get me in trouble if the old biddies find this stuff in my drawer." Liam laughed.

"What won't they let you have in here?" Matt asked.

"Pretty much everything." Liam winked at him and patted Erin's knee. "But I've got my own secret supply line." Erin pulled the last item from the bag and held it up for both men to see.

"Ah, bless you, my girl. 'Tis my favorite brand of Irish whiskey." Liam glanced at Matt. "I like a wee nip before sleep takes me."

"And a wee nip in his morning coffee and a wee nip—"

"Hush now, Erin. Don't tell all my secrets."

A knock on the door brought a flurry of activity as Erin grabbed the items, put them back in the bag and slipped it into a drawer of the nightstand.

"Come in," Liam called out.

One of the aforementioned old biddies breezed into the room with a blood pressure cuff and a small paper cup of pills. "Time for your medicine, Mr. O'Roarke."

The old man grumbled while Erin offered a smile to the aide.

"We'll get out of your way." She rose, and Matt followed her cue and stood. "I'll be back soon, Liam. Be nice to these wonderful people who take good care of you."

He waved at her to go away while he grumbled some more.

The aide laughed. "He just talks big to impress you, but when you or his wife aren't around, he's a sweetheart."

"Erin, wait," Liam said. "I nearly forgot to mention that your friend stopped by. Kept thinking I should know him from somewhere, but he said he only just arrived in town. Said his name was Allen. Nice enough fellow, and I was glad for the company. Told him he could stop by anytime. Wanted to thank you for sending him my way."

"Allen? I don't recall… What did he look like?"

"About as tall as Matt there, beard and mustache. Poor guy looked like he lost a fight, had a scar across his face."

Matt grabbed Erin by the elbow when she teetered. Her face had gone sheet white and her eyes rounded like saucers.

"What's the matter, my girl?" Liam asked.

Erin took a deep breath. "Nothing. Just a bit hungry, is all. What did this man say to you, Liam?"

"Oh, nothing much. We just chatted about this and that. Nothing of real consequence."

"Okay. Thanks for telling me. You'll let me know if he comes back again, won't you?"

"Sure, if that's what you want."

"I do. You know how much I enjoy keeping tabs on you," she said, her voice shaky, a false smile plastered on her face.

Liam appeared not to notice. "Ack! You're worse than my wife."

"I'm telling her you said that."

"Nah, you'd never betray me like that."

Erin's smile was genuine this time. "You're right, I wouldn't. See you next time."

"Sit still," the aide scolded, "or I'll never get this cuff on you."

"Hate having my blood pressure taken. That cuff of yours pinches." Liam's complaints continued.

Matt held Erin's arm as he led her out of the room and down the hall. "You okay on your own?" he asked when they reached the front door.

She nodded.

"Wait here." Matt went to the desk and spoke to the receptionist, telling her that Alex Townsend should not be allowed into the facility again under any name. He promised to email them a picture of the man within the hour.

"Thank you," Erin said to Matt as they left the building. Then without speaking further, she went to the passenger side of his truck and waited obediently for him to unlock it. She got in, buckled up, then manually locked the passenger door.

After he jogged around to the driver's side and climbed in, Matt cranked the engine and headed out of the parking lot. "Anyplace else you need to go?"

"No. Just take me home." She leaned back against the headrest and closed her eyes.

It seemed he wouldn't need to revisit security protocols with her after all. Alex had taken care of that for him by scaring the living daylights out of her, and now Matt burned with a sudden need to punch something.

Something like Alex Townsend's face.

Chapter Four

Alex Townsend rode the borrowed Harley back to his friend's place, where he was crashing for now. His visit to the old guy in the rest home, so soon after confronting Erin, was just to let her know how accessible her friends were. He didn't want to *really* threaten anybody. At least, not yet. Just a reminder that time flies.

He wouldn't be mooching off his friends from the bar for long, though. As soon as Erin did what needed doing, he'd be leaving Texas in his rearview mirror, just like the song.

And she needed to do it fast, because Cowboy didn't bluff.

Alex hadn't thought twice about sharing details of his crimes in prison. Even exaggerated them to build his reputation. But his last cellmate, Cowboy, had latched on to the story of the stolen jewelry from Winston, and he wanted it.

Explaining the loot was missing didn't matter to Cowboy. When he wanted something, he got it.

And all of a sudden, Cowboy had the name and address of Alex's ma, who was raising his son.

The kid's baby mama had handed a then-twenty-year-old Alex an unnamed bundle of dirty diapers on her way out the door, and Alex handed it to his ma. But during all that handing off, he'd named the kid Justin because it sounded like a smart person's name, and they were his favorite brand of boots.

Alex hadn't seen Justin since, but he'd sent money home whenever he could. The kid must be close to fourteen by now. But he wouldn't get much older if Alex didn't get the stolen goods to Cowboy's man outside the prison. The man willing to wipe out two generations of Townsends at Cowboy's command.

And Alex wasn't about to let his son, or his ma for that matter, die because Cowboy didn't get what he wanted.

Chapter Five

Well before dawn the next morning, Erin crept out of her room, her feet covered in socks. After a quick and quiet detour to the bathroom, she tiptoed past Matt's open door. This was her chance to sneak away and search for the stolen goods without him knowing. A trace of guilt spread through her about the guest room's condition yesterday when he arrived. But with no advance notice of an incoming bodyguard, she'd had no reason to organize the room. And yet, the guilt didn't evaporate, because she wouldn't have organized it even if she'd known he planned to stay with her.

Passive-aggressive much?

Frustrated, Erin grabbed her jacket and boots, eased open the front door and slipped through, closing it behind her without a sound. The predawn chill sank into her bones before she could get her jacket buttoned up. By the time she stepped off the porch and into her boots, her entire body yearned for the warmth of hot coffee, but there was no time today.

Yes, she was frustrated, because deep down guilt was needling her for more than just the condition of Matt's room.

Right out of the gate, she was breaking Bodyguard

Rule Number One: don't go anywhere without him. But despite the additional guilt brought on by sneaking away, she knew it wouldn't stop her. Her mind set on finding the missing jewels, she couldn't let her mother's hired babysitter interfere with that.

In the barn, Erin worked as fast as she could to saddle Shadow, one of her own horses. With the door closed, she worked beneath the overhead lights to attach her pickax and folding shovel to the saddlebag. The same tools she'd stealth-ordered from the hardware store the previous day. She said a silent thank-you to Hank for leaving the delivery in the barn, unopened.

Flashlight in her pocket, she turned off the overhead lights and led Shadow out through the barn's rear door. The inky darkness made it too dangerous to ride, so she and the horse would walk until her eyes adjusted. When the sky lightened a bit, she'd mount up and they'd pick up the pace. Although going off by herself broke Matt's number one rule, she made a mental one-sided compromise with him that seemed fair: she wouldn't leave the property.

Last night before sleep finally took her, Erin had wracked her brain, thinking of places where one of Alex's accomplices might have hidden the stolen goods. She'd finally settled on an area along the eastern property line of the Montgomery Ranch that sat far from all the post-robbery activity at the house, but close enough to the county road behind the property for quick access.

Shifting the loot back onto the property would have been a clever move, not that any of Alex's cohorts possessed much intelligence. But the police search had focused on public land. Whoever took the haul may have figured sneaking back onto the ranch was a risk worth taking.

Darkness slowed her progress, but Erin was determined to stick to the dirt road that cut across the property from front to back. When the dawn's light peeked above the horizon, she'd veer to the east. Drawing images of that part of the ranch to mind, she mentally pinpointed possible dig sites.

"Where the hell do you think you're going?"

Erin screeched. Her heart came to a full stop, then roared back to life with the thunderous booming of a kettledrum. She whipped around to find Matt ten feet behind her, shining a flashlight at her face.

Damn it!

She slapped her hand over her pounding heart. "You really need to learn how to approach people without scaring the daylights out of them. And would you get that light out of my eyes?"

"I asked you a question." Matt lowered the flashlight, but only a little.

Asserting his dominance, was he? Erin shone her flashlight in his direction to let him know two could play this game. The scowl on his handsome face brought her a small sense of satisfaction.

Matt shaded his eyes to block the light. "You can't sneak off like this. I thought you understood that."

"I'm not sneaking. I'm going for an early morning ride. I like watching the sunrise from on top of a horse. Besides, it's not like I left the property."

"Remind me where it was that Alex first approached you?" Matt asked. "Oh, yeah. *On* your property."

He certainly had her there.

"Come on." Matt motioned with his light. "We're going back."

Erin's huff of frustration formed a white cloud in the chilled air. She needed to stop letting him get under her skin. At the same time, she managed to remind herself what was at stake. Her parents. Liam. Hank. Tommy. They might all be in danger if she didn't find the missing haul, and now she'd blown her best chance to hunt for the loot. Even worse, Matt would now be more vigilant than ever.

Her brain spun with ideas of what to do. Stewing in anger or arguing with him wouldn't help. Erin drew in a deep breath. Since she wasn't going to give up hunting for the loot, and she doubted she'd get another chance to do it alone, she had no choice but to bring him along.

She tugged Shadow's reins. "I'm not going back. I'm going for a ride, just like I said. Come if you want, but it's a long walk."

She half expected him to stop her, but he stepped up to the other side of Shadow's head and walked with her. "What's your horse's name?"

"This is Shadow." Erin ran her hand over the mare's withers. "The palomino in the barn is Blaze."

After a few more steps, Matt asked his original question again. "What's so doggone important that you're willing to risk your life for?"

In the misty darkness of the quiet morning, separated only by a horse, the sense of intimacy surprised Erin. Intimate, and yet anonymous, like having the privacy screen of a confessional booth between them. She may as well come clean with him. "There's another reason I wanted to ride this morning."

"You don't say."

She ignored the twinge of sarcasm in his voice. "I'm trying to find the stolen jewelry."

Only the clop-clop of Shadow's hooves broke the silence.

Then, "Let the authorities handle that."

"You don't understand."

"Then explain it to me."

Erin pressed her lips together. She wasn't used to explaining herself to anyone. But like it or not, figuring out a way to make this work with Matt was imperative. "When Alex was here, he threatened to hurt the people I care about. That's why he paid a visit to Liam."

"How is Liam involved in this? How did Alex know who you visited?"

"Liam attended the party that night. He's the man Alex sent to the hospital after pistol-whipping him."

"That's why his name sounded familiar. I must've seen it when I skimmed the police report." Matt reached for the reins, and Erin let them drop, curious to see what he intended. He brought Shadow to a gentle halt, along with Erin. "Has Liam lived at Hidden Oaks since that night?"

Matt's incredulity almost distracted her from his subtle attempt to end her hunt. Almost. She allowed him to turn her back toward the barn. Well, he'd need a horse if he came with her. No harm in letting him think, for the moment anyway, that he was winning their war of wills.

"Alex hit him so hard, it caused a stroke. Left Liam partially paralyzed, and he needs more care than his wife can handle at home. They're wealthy, so at first they tried keeping him home with private nurses. But he still had a lot of anger. The nurses kept quitting. His wife believed

Hidden Oaks would be a good solution until he calmed down. But by the time he had, they'd both developed their own routines and decided not to rock the boat."

"So that's why you visit him? Out of guilt?"

The disdain in Matt's voice made her angry about his presumption. But how could she be and stay honest with herself? "It started out that way, sure. And every time I went, he raged at me." Erin kicked a rock in her path. "I deserved it. Eventually, though, his anger faded. It's taken years to develop the relationship we have now."

"Okay, Liam. Got it. One box checked." Matt continued leading them toward the barn. "But let's circle back to that night. I'm curious about something. After the heist, an anonymous call notified the authorities. EMT and the police arrived within minutes of that initial 911 call. But the report states that someone cut the landline, and your gang took everyone's cell phones."

Erin's posture stiffened, and in the pale gray light of the cold dawn she held his gaze without blinking. "They weren't *my* gang."

"Semantics. And not the point. What I find odd is no one had access to a phone, yet someone reported the crime almost immediately after it happened."

Erin gave a noncommittal shrug.

The deep creases across his forehead softened. "You called the police, didn't you?"

Interesting that Matt deduced what everyone else had missed. "No one was supposed to get hurt. I didn't even know anyone had a gun." Her throat tightened at the memory of Liam lying crumpled on the floor, blood pooling around him from the gash on his head, his face as pale as a sun-bleached skull. Afterward, what had kept her awake at night was knowing that if she'd possessed even half a brain back then, she could have prevented it. Matt was right. She did have guilt. A mountain of it.

"Alex had given us all burner phones, and Liam needed help. I called as soon as the others left the woods."

Her gaze clouded over as horrible memories of that night continued to rush forward. The people she'd known her whole life, their faces filled with terror. The shouts, the screams, overturned tables, broken china and crystal. And then there'd been Alex.

"I'd never seen Alex like that before," she said. "He swore to me that no one would get hurt. But once inside the house, he became a monster. He pistol-whipped Liam just to show everyone he meant business, that they'd better do what he said or else. I was afraid Liam would die. What else could I do but call 911?"

Matt's tone softened. "Did you tell the police you made the call?"

"No."

"It might have helped your case if they'd known that."

Erin's eyes refocused. The way he said it, the look on his face... She could almost think it was empathy.

"That's not why I did it."

"How'd you get involved with Alex in the first place?"

"As a teenager, my mom wanted me to play the socialite's daughter and assist her with charity galas. But I had a rebellious streak and instead volunteered at one of the charities she supported." Erin smiled to herself, remembering her mother's reaction.

Matt snorted.

"What?"

"You and I have different concepts of a teenage rebel."

"I'll have you know, rebels come in all shapes and sizes." She straightened her back, clenching her teeth. Why did this man make her want to argue every little point? "But I thought you wanted to know how I met Alex."

"Sorry. Go ahead."

"As I started to explain, Alex showed up a few months later, also as a volunteer. He was charismatic, and when he showed an interest in someone, they fell under his spell." Erin rubbed her hand over Shadow's neck. "My mother ran off any boys I wanted to date, setting me up instead with the sons of those in her social circle."

"What? You didn't like the rich boys?"

"You can't help it, can you?"

Matt flinched. "What are you talking about?"

"Is it part of your job description to constantly needle me, or do you just enjoy it? Maybe both?"

Putting his hand to his heart, he said, "I'm sorry. Really. Continue, please."

Sucker that she was, Erin chose to believe in his sincerity. "Mainly, I didn't want to turn into my mother." She shuddered at the thought. "Anyway, back to Alex. While a volunteer, he also made friends with a few guys who worked there. I found out later they were on probation and working there as part of a community service program."

"Were you the only girl in the group?"

Erin ducked her head to hide the blush warming her cheeks. "Yes. Alex cultivated a relationship with me separately at first, then started taking me to the bar where he met with the others. He argued, and very convincingly, that less waste on an expensive charity gala would mean more money for the people who needed it. What can I say? I was in love. Or at least thought I was. Plus, I'd witnessed firsthand what my mother shelled out for one of her parties, so I completely bought his argument. He made it sound romantic, like a Robin Hood caper, and I was too young and naive to see it for what it was." She scoffed. "Obviously, the other three knew no money from the stolen goods would make it any farther than their own pockets, but I didn't."

She fell quiet then, unsure of herself. Other than her initial statement to the police, she'd never talked about the burglary with anyone but her lawyer. Never spoken about it aloud in such a detached, fact-based way. Strange that Matt could ask a couple of questions and parts of her sordid past came pouring out.

"What exactly was Alex's plan?" Matt asked.

"You read the police report."

"I'm sure it's difficult to talk about, but I'd like to hear it from you."

She massaged the back of her neck. "Fine. My parents had a charity gala planned. Alex had magnetic signs made for the charity's van we, uh…borrowed, that made it look like one of the catering vans."

"And that's how you got in?"

Erin paused. "Well, that, and me knowing the gate code. My job was to drive the van. We met at a spot in the woods that Alex had chosen, where the guys hid their bikes. I'd told my parents I wouldn't be home for the party, and we all wore ski masks. I waited by the door while Alex and two of the others collected everyone's jewelry, money and phones and the fourth guy emptied all the women's purses into a bag. There was no one to stop us as we drove back to the woods. They transferred the phones and wallets to one bag that Alex kept with him. We hid the bag of jewelry in a hole already dug, then they all took off in different directions on their motorcycles. I removed the magnetic signs and hid them in some bushes, then I was supposed to drive the van back to the charity."

"But the police stopped you at one of the roadblocks."

She nodded.

"And that happened soon after you left the woods?"

"Not too long after."

"Why didn't any of the others get stopped by roadblocks?"

Erin sighed. "I headed into town, to the charity, and the cops had *just* set up the roadblock. The others took back roads away from town."

Matt appeared to be making mental notes, and then his tone changed. "Since you were the last to leave, you could have moved the jewelry before you drove away."

"Yeah, right." Erin laughed. "I'm the one who told the police about the hiding place."

"Misdirection. You tell them where the original spot was only after you hide the stuff somewhere else." He shrugged. "You have to admit, it's a possibility."

Erin felt his eyes on her, watching for her reaction. "So you think I'm lying about the loot, and I'm going through all this, this charade, for…what? Fun?"

"Think about it." Matt held up a hand and began ticking off items on his fingers. "You didn't want a bodyguard. You just tried to sneak away. You didn't tell me you were going to go look for the stolen goods. Hell, you didn't even tell me you *planned* on looking for them. Not a lot in there to make you believable."

Though he spoke the truth, his words stung. "Believe

me or not. Doesn't matter to me. But then tell me this. Why would I be sneaking off to find the loot if I already have it?"

"Possibly to throw everyone off. Or maybe you just want to move it again. To a safer spot this time. And that's why you didn't want me with you."

"Think what you want. But heads up, Mr. Bodyguard. I *am* going to be looking for the loot, so either get out of my way or put on your spurs and grab a shovel."

They resumed their walk to the barn in silence.

After a few minutes, Matt said, "Okay, say for the sake of argument I believe you and you don't have the stuff. And let's even say that after ten years, you're somehow able to miraculously find this pot of gold. What then? Hand half of it to Alex and keep the rest? Give it all to him so the others won't come after you when they get out?"

And there it was. Judgment once again imbued with his disdainful tone. Erin finally had him figured out. Matt seemed incapable of forgiveness, as his blatant disapproval of her past made clear. "I have no control over what you think, but just to set the record straight, I intend to turn it in to the police. If they have it, there's no reason for Alex to harass me any longer." Erin added in a biting tone, "But I really appreciate your high opinion of me."

"What I think doesn't matter."

"You got that straight."

Matt drew in a sharp breath, then let it out. "Look. We got off to a rocky start. What do you say to me helping you search for the jewelry if you'll agree to wait for full light? Maybe until after I've had some coffee and breakfast."

Erin nodded. Although grateful he'd agreed to help, her ire still simmered. True, her past was against her.

And she'd snuck away and omitted telling him about her plan to find the loot. But one thing she'd never been was a liar. And for some reason, it was important to prove that to him before this whole thing was over.

By the time they finished a quick breakfast and Matt filled two thermoses with hot coffee, the sun was hard at work burning off the ground fog. In his professional opinion, finding the loot was about as likely as a blizzard in Los Angeles, but if nothing else, it would keep Erin close while giving him a chance to map out a good-sized portion of the property.

"Come on." Erin's eagerness to get going annoyed him.

He zipped his jacket, grabbed the thermoses and followed her outside. As he watched her sashay toward the barn, he replayed one portion of their earlier conversation. She'd surprised him with her plan to turn in the stolen jewelry instead of giving it to Alex. Matt frowned. He'd been burned before, so he'd believe that if and when it happened.

As far as her overall character was concerned, the jury was still out on that, but he conceded that perhaps he had judged her without knowing all the facts.

Erin hadn't unsaddled her horse before they ate, and as Matt followed her into the barn now, he realized this meant trouble for him. With Shadow's reins looped over a post, she walked to the third stall down and opened the gate. Patting the neck of the gold horse who must be Blaze, Erin gave her a quick brushing and led her from the stall. She grabbed another set of reins and fit the bit into the horse's mouth, then threw a blanket across the broad back before reaching for a saddle.

Matt rushed to intercept her. In a casual tone, he said, "Why don't we just walk? I'll carry the tools."

Cinching the saddle straps, Erin smirked. "This is an eight-hundred-acre ranch, and we're going to a section on the far southeast side."

Matt was a whiz with numbers, but he didn't know the calculation of acres to miles off the top of his head. "Still—"

By now, Erin was reaching for Shadow's reins. "We'll be out searching all day. I'd prefer riding, though you can walk if you want. Of course, you won't be able to keep up. But trust me, that won't bother me one bit."

"I guess you can't help it either."

Her head cocked in confusion. "Help what?"

"Needling me. Just part of your charming personality, I guess." Matt enjoyed the sour look that crossed her face when her words were thrown back at her.

She surprised him again with her measured response. "Touché." She dug into her jacket pocket and brought out some chunks of carrots, which she offered Shadow. Those large square teeth chomped on the treat as Erin grabbed Blaze's reins and offered the gold horse some carrots as well. Then she led both animals outside.

Despite the crisp morning, Matt began to sweat. "Why don't we drive? We can take my truck."

"Very kind of you to offer, but the terrain where we're going isn't conducive to vehicles like your truck, even if they're four-wheel drive. And both of the ranch's off-road utility vehicles are in the maintenance shed, you know, being maintained." She gave him a dry smile as she loaded the saddlebags on both horses with tools, emergency supplies and the thermoses.

Apparently, his attempts at disguising his discomfort weren't succeeding, and Erin was enjoying herself way too much at his expense.

"Besides which—" she went on, swinging up onto Shadow in one smooth motion "—the maintenance shed is in the opposite direction from where we're headed, way over on the northeast side of the ranch, near the stable and main bunkhouse."

"Wait. There's another bunkhouse and stable?" This was something he would need to inspect for possible safety concerns.

Her laugh hung in the chilled air. "Where do you think all the rest of our horses are? And where our ranch hands stay, except for Hank, of course? And the grazing pastures are that way, too."

"I thought this was it." He waved his hand to indicate the barn behind them.

"An eight-hundred-acre horse ranch with only two horses?"

"Three horses. What about the black?"

"Redemption is a client's horse. I'm helping him recover from an injury." Erin motioned Matt toward the gold horse. "Mount up."

Damn it. The moment of truth. Matt refused to swipe at the perspiration dripping down the sides of his face. "Look, I've never ridden a horse before."

Not entirely true. He *had* ridden a horse. Once. For about two minutes. But he'd been a kid, and the ornery beast had reared up. Matt had screamed bloody murder and tried to leap off, but his fright spooked the animal and it careened down the trail. Matt's foot got stuck sideways in the stirrup. Before the instructor could get to him, he fell off and landed in a fresh, stinking pile of horse manure. The other kids had still been laughing at him as the bus took them back to school.

All in all, not the worst thing that could've happened, but trauma at that age left scars. To this day, horses petrified him.

Erin's eyes widened. "Never?"

Matt shook his head.

Erin blew out a breath as she walked Shadow over to the gold horse. "Blaze is calm, gentle and absolutely won't buck you off. All you need to do is hang on." She leaned down, grabbed Blaze's reins and handed them to Matt. Then, looking down at him like the Queen of Boone County, she said, "Take hold of the reins in your left hand, up near her neck."

Matt did as she instructed.

"Good. Now put your left foot in the stirrup." Erin gave him an encouraging smile.

Lifting his left leg, Matt tried slipping his toe into the stirrup. But Blaze sidestepped, and his boot slid off the metal.

"Come on, Mr. Bodyguard. We don't have all day."

"Hold your horses." He wasn't amused when Erin laughed at the unintended pun. The only thing that kept him from snapping at her was his concern about provoking her. She might decide to take off and leave him in the dust. Literally.

"Hold the stirrup with your right hand if you need to."

He didn't need to. He didn't even need her instructions. All those years ago, he'd gotten *on* the horse just fine. Getting *off* had been the problem. And he'd let that humiliating and painful experience fester into a phobia.

Matt went for the stirrup again, and this time his boot slid in. Before Erin could tell him what to do next, he swung his right leg over and settled into the saddle. His anxiety settled in too, gripping his guts in a fist of apprehension, because at some point he'd need to get off the horse.

"That was great. You look like you were born to ride." Erin gave him a playful wink. He liked her this way. Not the part about him being the target of her teasing, but the way her joking softened the lines of her face and added a sparkle to her eyes. With the soft light of the rising sun illuminating wisps of her hair like a halo, she looked downright angelic. Beautiful, actually. And that made her dangerous.

"Yeah, right."

She stopped poking fun at him as they took off down the dirt road at a slow walk. "Try holding just the reins."

Matt glanced down at his hands, gripping the saddle horn as well as the reins. "I'm good."

Erin's mouth kicked up at the corners with a smile she couldn't hide. "Seriously, let go of the horn. Between the reins and your thighs, you'll have more control. And it's safer."

Safer. That, more than the smile, made him tighten his hold on the reins and lift his hands from the saddle. When Blaze tossed her head and snorted, Matt tensed, reins still in a death grip. He wiped sweat off his forehead with his jacket sleeve, then grabbed the horn again. *To hell with what she said.*

Erin blocked his path, stopped and brought her phone out of her pocket. "Let go of the horn, or I'll take pictures of my big, strong bodyguard who can't ride a horse."

Just what he needed. A social media hit to his professional reputation. "Put the phone away."

"I will, but only if you let go of the horn. For real, it's the only way you'll learn how to ride." Erin's mouth set in a firm line. "Or do you want to be afraid of horses the rest of your life?"

Blaze shook her head, snorting at Matt's tight hold.

Matt mimicked the sound but did as Erin demanded.

With a satisfied nod, Erin put away her phone and clicked her tongue. Both horses started moving again.

Matt had planned to get a look at the safeguarding measures implemented at the rest of the ranch's operations, but Erin made it clear they were headed in a different direction. Maybe he'd have time later in the day. If not, he might need to have Blake, the security system installer Nate used on a contract basis, come back out and do the inspection. The ranch had a lot of real estate to cover.

For now, Erin might be able to provide some info. "Why are the big stable and bunkhouse so far away from your parents' house? It doesn't make sense to have a mini setup where you live and all the rest at the back of the property."

"This ranch has three purposes, at least for my mom." Erin's huff of exasperation reeked of sarcasm.

Man, she really doesn't seem to like her mother.

She lifted a hand, her index finger jutting straight up. "Number one, convey wealth and status. Number two, breed, raise and board horses, and number three, train dressage horses for competition." She rolled her eyes. "Mother used to compete. I think she hangs on to the world of dressage to retain her illusion of youth." Erin scoffed. "Or should I say her *delusion* of youth?"

Oh, yes. The mommy issues came in loud and clear. He'd need to tiptoe around that minefield. "I've heard of dressage, but I don't really know what it is."

"It's a style of riding where the rider uses invisible communication to make the horse go through a series of distinct movements. When done correctly, the harmony between the horse and rider is a beautiful thing to watch. Anyway, the ranch exists because my mom wanted it," she said. "My dad lives to make money and to make my mom happy. Not sure of the order of those two things, but when they planned the layout of the ranch, the only thing my dad requested was that the horse business wasn't in his daily line of sight. He doesn't hate the animals. He just doesn't want them front and center. Personally, I think he dislikes the smell, which is crazy. Nothing beats the scent of horses and hay."

"Then why is your barn, corral and bunkhouse near the front?"

"My place sits behind and to the side of the main house. You can't see it from the front of the house, and the house is angled so the back of it doesn't face it either. Approaching the property and main house, I'm far enough away that the buildings aren't noticeable unless you're looking for them." Erin led the way along a narrow path between towering live oaks. "It was originally built so my mom could train a few dressage horses without having to cross the whole ranch. Eventually, she quit training and assigned me the job."

"So why, with that enormous house, do you live in the bunkhouse?"

"To get away from my mom."

That answer didn't surprise Matt.

"She micromanages every aspect of my life and has since...well, you know. Made sense at the time, since I don't have the best track record when it comes to making good decisions. After the robbery, I didn't trust myself at all. And for a while, after the case was adjudicated, it was easier to let her have her way." She shivered, but Matt doubted it was from the morning chill. "Until one day I just couldn't breathe. So I moved to the bunkhouse."

The horses splashed across a shallow stream.

Matt surveyed the terrain. Fields of winter-dead wild grass stretched away to the west. To the east, the trees grew sparser and the ground vegetation gave way to dirt and rocks. "What makes you think the loot might be buried on your property, and why out here?"

"There've been rumors over the years that Alex or one of the other men doubled back and moved the loot right after the robbery. I know it wasn't me, and I think we can cross Alex off the list since he thinks I have it. That leaves Billy Jensen, who's dead, Brad Parker and Kevin Moore. I can only assume Alex has already talked to Brad and Kevin, especially since they had their prison sentences extended. So, my best guess is that one of them lied, or Jensen moved it but was killed before Alex could question him. It really doesn't matter who moved it, only that it was moved. And whoever did it couldn't get back to retrieve it."

"Except you."

Erin turned her head and narrowed her eyes on Matt. "Except I didn't. And I'm not going to say that again. Got it?"

"Got it." Although she could be lying, somehow Matt didn't think so.

She loosened the reins and Shadow continued at a somewhat faster pace. A pace that Matt didn't care for. Not one bit. His backside was bouncing up and down, hitting the stiff leather of the saddle each time with a hard smack, like swats he'd taken in some of the foster homes he'd lived in while growing up. How the heck did Erin make trotting look so easy and natural?

She moved out in front, telegraphing her displeasure with Matt's speed in a clear message. "So, the way I see it, if no one retrieved it, then it could still be where it was left."

"*Could* be. But someone unrelated to the crime might have found it. Hell, someone who never even heard about the crime could have happened upon it."

"I guess that's possible," Erin conceded. "But not likely if it's on our property. Besides, none of the jewelry ever turned up in a pawnshop. And if one of Alex's guys moved it, then this would have been the perfect hiding place since the cops focused their search in the area where the jewelry had originally been hidden. They didn't search the ranch, because who in their right mind would chance coming back to the scene of the crime? But whoever took it could have planned on waiting until the commotion died down, then slipping back onto the property to recover it later."

"I still say it's a long shot, but my money's on Jensen."

"Jensen was killed within a month of the robbery, ironically while robbing a convenience store. How's that for karma? If he knew where the loot was, why would he do something so stupid?"

"A lot of *ifs* in your thinking, which is why I think this

hunt of yours is a colossal waste of time. Not to mention leaving you exposed to any number of potential threats."

Erin glared at him from over her shoulder. "I don't remember asking for your opinion, and it's not like you have anything more important to do right now. Or do you? Maybe you want to quit. There's always that option."

Matt's silence answered her.

"That's what I thought," she muttered.

After a long, excruciating ride, they approached a wooded area interspersed with large boulders, rock piles and scrub brush. Erin dismounted in one smooth move and wrapped her horse's reins around a tree limb. Matt stayed in the saddle, his clammy hands tightly wrapped around the horn again.

"You're going to have to get down if you plan on helping me search." Erin's lips curled into a wry smile. Apparently, her temper had cooled, and she was back to mocking him. "Or have you become enamored of horses and never want to leave the saddle?"

"Getting down seems the more difficult choice."

With the sun above the horizon, Erin squinted up at him. "It's not. You just do everything you did to get on the horse, but in the opposite order."

"Gee, why didn't I think of that?"

"Oh, come on, you big baby. Kids can do this."

Some kids can. Matt exhaled in resignation, then swung his right foot over the horse's back and toward the ground. But his childhood nightmare returned to haunt him. The toe of his left boot slid forward. With Matt caught in the stirrup. Blaze, curse the beast, refused to stand still. She moved sideways, apparently trying to get away from her rider. Matt held on to the horn for dear life, his left foot firmly stuck while his body hung down the horse's flank, his right foot hopping awkwardly on the ground. He and Blaze did a circular five-legged dance to the tune of Erin's laughter.

"A little help here?"

Still chuckling, Erin grabbed Blaze's reins and, with one word, commanded the mare to stand still. "Get back on her, then when you dismount, don't tip your left foot forward."

Matt followed her instructions and ended up standing on two legs instead of sitting in the dirt. Or worse, in another pile of steaming manure.

"You're doing pretty well with the riding itself, at least at a walk. We can increase your speed gradually. But you need to work on your unhorsing." She gave him an encouraging smile. "Don't worry. If I can teach Tommy Barrows how to ride, I can teach you."

Matt walked Blaze to the tree and wrapped the reins around a branch, repeating her last words in a sarcastic tone too soft to hear. At least this time he'd only bruised his ego.

And while Erin reminded him of his bruised ego with good-natured teasing throughout the day as they poked into rock formations and dug around trees, it didn't bother him nearly as much as he thought it would.

Go figure.

Chapter Six

When they reached the barn, Erin dismounted and took Blaze's reins from Matt. "I'll just hold on to these until you have both feet on the ground." She tried her best to keep a straight face, but the smile playing at the corners of her mouth won.

"Very funny." Matt swung one leg over the horse and managed to get his other foot out of the stirrup without an encore performance of his and Blaze's five-legged boogie.

"You're making progress." Erin handed the reins of both horses to him, then opened the barn doors. "I'll make a cowboy out of you yet."

She replaced Shadow's bridle with a halter and lead rope and knotted it to a tie ring, pleased to see Matt studying and then copying her every move with Blaze. She handed him a brush and showed him how to use it by keeping her hand over his for the first few strokes, ignoring the tingles and sparks in her fingers.

"As you brush, examine every part of her. Look for rubs or chafing from the saddle. Feel her legs for cuts or bumps." Erin returned to Shadow and began brushing. "Between how cold it is outside and how slow we were walking, they won't need much of a cooldown period."

"So what do we do after brushing and checking them over?"

"Give them some hay in their stalls. It was a long day, even moving slowly, so I don't want to feed them grain right away." She glanced at Matt, who seemed to almost enjoy working with Blaze. At least his fear of horses was lessening.

Once the horses were squared away, Erin walked with Matt to the bunkhouse. "Think we need to move the search off the ranch tomorrow?"

But Matt didn't answer, his attention focused on the building's roofline. "Excellent. Nate had the cameras installed." He turned and looked back at the barn, a smile spreading across his face. "And he had enough in stock to send extras."

Erin pulled her gaze from the unfamiliar protrusions adorning the cabin and followed Matt's line of sight. "Why are there cameras on my barn?" Her fingers curled into fists as her mood took a dive.

"I just told you, Nate must have sent extras." Matt climbed the porch steps.

The frustration of once again not being in control, the anger of losing even more privacy, burned through Erin like a river of lava. "I didn't give you permission to install cameras all over the place. You never even asked."

"You must've been too busy trying to think of a way to get rid of me yesterday to pay attention when I took an inventory of the security measures that needed to be beefed up." Matt chuckled.

Erin joined him on the porch, despair drilling a hole in her gut as she noticed even more cameras attached to the porch roof, at least one facing the front door. "Look,

I appreciate you wanting to make sure I'm safe. But this is overkill. I don't want cameras on me every time I step out of my house."

"Once this job is over, I'll gladly remove everything we've installed if you no longer want it." One corner of his mouth lifted into a sly grin. "But for now, it all stays. Come on, let's see what Blake did on the inside."

"Who's Blake?" Erin asked.

"The guy Nate uses to install alarm systems."

"I swear, if there's so much as one camera *inside* my home—"

Matt punched in the code and opened the front door. "Relax. No cameras inside." He moved through the rooms, checking the windows, new dead bolts on the doors and everything else he'd had installed without her consent.

While Erin paid attention to everything Matt was looking at, she also checked the ceiling corners and beams for cameras. When she glanced again at Matt, he stood there, grinning.

"What'd I tell you? No cameras inside." Matt held his arms wide.

Erin planted her fists on her hips. "Hmm. I wouldn't put it past you to hide one of those pinhole cameras or baby monitor ones. I should probably check to make sure there aren't any cute stuffed animals sitting around."

Matt barked out a laugh. "You watch a lot of true-crime shows?"

"I know those things exist." Erin examined everything that faced the front door, figuring that was the view Matt would most likely be interested in. "Are the cameras outside to watch for someone trying to break in or to watch for me trying to sneak out?"

Matt, confirming the new thumb locks prevented the windows from opening, glanced at her. "It's always a good thing when you can kill two birds with one stone."

"Hmph." Erin toed off her boots and dropped onto the couch. She didn't like losing even more privacy, but she understood the need for the cameras—she just wouldn't let Matt know she understood.

"I really can't see checking much more of your property for the loot," Matt answered her earlier question as he sat near her. "Tell me about where you all took the stolen stuff when you left your parents' party."

"Alex had already picked out a spot in the woods. Not too far from here so the stuff could be stashed quickly. Into the trees, a ways in from the road so no one in passing cars would see us, but there's a turnoff where I drove the van in to hide it."

"And you don't know what any of the guys did after you all left the woods?"

Erin shook her head. "They arrested Alex and Brad in the wee hours of the next morning, and brought in Kevin not long after that. Somehow, Billy evaded all the blockades and disappeared."

Matt tapped a finger against his chin. "What if the cop who was supposed to retrieve it only *said* the hole was empty?" Matt leaned forward, his forearms on his knees. "What if *he* took it?"

"He didn't."

"How can you be so sure?"

"The Winston PD got one body camera way back when they first became popular in the US. They wanted to make sure it was worth spending the money before they bought more of them." Erin closed her eyes in shame, recalling the time spent being interrogated. "Chief Simpson told the cop to wear it so they could test its efficiency in the dark."

"There goes that theory." Matt drummed his fingers on his knee. "But even if we only have your gang to work with, we're still narrowing it down. If Brad or Kevin re-hid the stuff, where would they have put it?"

"Would you please stop referring to them as *my gang*?" Erin glared at him before she picked up her phone and opened a map app. Matt slid closer to her and leaned in to view the screen over her shoulder.

"Here's where the stuff was hidden first." She tapped her screen, dropping a pin at the spot in the woods. "The police arrested them here and here." She dropped two more pins at locations on the far side of town.

Matt stayed quiet, focusing on the map. "If we concentrate on the areas between the woods and where the cops picked them up, that will narrow down our hunting ground."

Erin nodded. "At least to start."

"We can do a little more research in the morning about the geography of our target areas, and then I'd like to start out at the original burial spot." Matt tapped her phone screen to indicate the pin.

"Sounds good to me." Erin's stomach growled. "I'm starving."

"That pizza I bought is in the freezer."

"That'll work." Erin stood and stretched, then headed for the kitchen. "I'll turn on the oven, then you can put the pizza in while I take a shower."

After checking the temperature and bake time on the pizza box, she opened the oven door before turning it on. She'd developed this habit after hiding some dirty dishes in the oven and forgetting about them. She never wanted to smell the reek of toxic fumes from melted plastic again. And cleaning up shattered glasses had not been fun.

Erin bent over for a quick peek inside. The oven light shone like a spotlight on something in the middle of the top rack. Something her mind refused to compute.

"Matt!" Not quite a scream, but loud and shrill.

In seconds, Matt stood by her side. "What?"

Erin pointed at the oven. "There's an eyeball in there."

Crouching, Matt looked inside, then grabbed a paper towel and brought out the item without leaving his fingerprints.

Tommy's latest find, the large marble he'd shown Matt yesterday, sat glued to the center of a white plate. The message, finger-painted in blood, circled the marble.

Tick Tick Tick

BEFORE MATT COULD say a word, Erin rushed to her phone. While it rang, he said, "Put it on speaker."

Tommy's mother picked up.

"Jill? It's Erin."

"Are you all right? You sound funny." Jill kept her voice low.

"I, um, can I speak with Tommy?" Erin eyed Matt, her face a picture of panic.

"He's already in bed. What's going on?"

Matt glanced at his watch, unaware of the late hour.

"This must sound strange, but I was wondering if he still has that marble he showed Matt in the store."

Jill let out a small laugh. "Well, yes it *does* sound strange, calling this late about a marble." The clink of ice cubes in a glass came through the phone. "And even stranger, that marble seems to have disappeared."

"How did it disappear?" Erin asked, sounding calmer.

"Well, Tommy was playing marbles on the front porch when I called him in to put on a warmer jacket. He couldn't have been in the house more than a minute or two, but when he went back out, he claimed that marble was gone. His whole marble collection was out there, but only that one disappeared." Ice clinked against glass again. "It probably just rolled into the bushes."

Matt met Erin's eyes as she raised her hands in a question: *Should she tell Jill what they found?*

Instead of speaking through Erin, Matt said, "Jill, this is Matt. Can we stop by to show you something? It'll only take a minute."

"I guess so. Y'all are starting to worry me."

"No need to worry," Erin said. "We'll see you soon." As soon as she ended the call, she glared at him. "Are you out of your mind? You want to show her what happened to his marble?"

"Of course not." Matt shook his head, surprised she would think that. "We need to show her a picture of Townsend so she can make sure he doesn't get anywhere near Tommy." He pulled a picture from the police file and put on his jacket.

Erin grabbed her coat, and Matt escorted her to his truck with one hand on her shoulder and the other on his gun.

"TOWNSEND IS TRYING to prove he can get to anyone you care about," Matt said as they left the Barrowses' house half an hour after they'd arrived.

"He's done more than try." The anger and bitterness in Erin's voice filled the truck. "He's gotten to Liam and gotten close to Tommy. You should be protecting everyone I know instead of me."

"You think Jill's going to be okay?"

"I hope so." Erin wrapped her arms around herself, as if more than the night air chilled her. "We definitely gave her a scare. At least she agreed to start using her alarm system again."

Matt snapped his fingers. "That reminds me." He tapped a button on the steering wheel. "Call Blake."

A deep voice came through the truck's audio system. "Hey, Matt. What's up?"

"I need you back at the Montgomery Ranch pronto. We need the digital locks for the bunkhouse and barn changed. Front gate, too."

"I didn't change any of those when I was there." Blake sounded wary. "Was I supposed to?"

"No, I didn't think it would be necessary." Matt blew out a frustrated breath. "When you were installing the equipment today, did you see anyone?"

"Just some guy named Hank. Said he was Ms. Montgomery's ranch hand. He offered to help, but you know we can't risk someone getting hurt." Based on the sounds of a car door closing and the engine starting, Blake was already on the move.

"Blake, this is Erin. What did this guy look like?"

"Hmm, probably in his thirties, slim, dark hair, beard and mustache. Looked like he broke his nose at least once." Road noise could be heard in the background now. "I'm on my way. Should be there in about twenty."

As soon as they heard the description, Erin grabbed

Matt's arm, her eyes wild. "We have to get to Hank's. Alex might have hurt him."

Stepping harder on the gas pedal, Matt spoke to the phone. "We might not be there when you arrive. Go ahead and change them, then send me the new codes." Erin directed him to continue past the Montgomery Ranch gate. "Do you carry, Blake?"

"Of course. And I never go out for a night job without Brutus."

"That's what you named your gun? Brutus?" Another mile, and Matt took a sharp right onto a minor road Erin pointed out to him.

A loud bark came through the phone.

"No, man. That's what I named my Rottweiler. He's a big baby, but if anyone even looks at me cross-eyed, he'll protect me or die trying."

"Watch your six. That guy at the house today was the jerk I'm protecting Erin from. We're on our way to check on the real Hank." Matt slowed and took another right turn. "I'll talk to you soon."

Hank's property was a small fraction of the size of the Montgomerys'. The dirt drive led to a small two-story house that looked less out of place in the countryside than the Montgomerys' modern mansion. White clapboard needed paint, a sun-faded red barn leaned a little.

He'd barely stopped in front of the house when Erin opened her door and jumped out.

"Erin!"

"Move faster or yell at me later. I'm not waiting for you to open my damn door." Even so, before she'd made it five steps toward the house, Matt was beside her, gun in hand as Erin bounded up the front steps and pounded on the front door.

Erin pounded again.

"Hold your horses. I'm on my way." Hank's distinctive, gravelly voice sounded from inside.

The door swung open and Erin almost fell into his arms. "Are you all right, Hank?" Her eyes scanned his body.

"Why wouldn't I be? Except for freezing my family jewels. Get in here before we're heating all of Winston on my dime." He opened the door wider and ushered them inside. "What in tarnation is going on?"

"Can we sit down? This may take a few minutes." When Hank nodded, Matt moved into the small living room on their right. He waited until Hank and Erin had taken seats on the small couch, then sat in the remaining chair. "Erin had a scare tonight and was worried that you might have been hurt."

Hank's head snapped back in surprise as he looked at Erin. "Why on earth would you think I got hurt?"

"Remember I told you about Matt's plan to install a security system at the ranch today?"

"Of course I do. That's why you told me to take the afternoon off." Hank glanced at Matt and stage-whispered, "She wanted to make sure I stayed out of the way while your man was working."

"That's not the reason." Erin frowned. "But Alex pretended to be you, and he walked right into my bunkhouse."

"We worried he might have made sure you wouldn't show up while he was impersonating you," Matt added.

Pulling his lips into a tight line, Hank muttered a string of curse words.

"I would never forgive myself if Alex hurt you while trying to get at me." Erin dragged her jacket sleeve across her eyes.

"Don't be foolish." Hank shook his head. "I've told you before, you're not responsible for what someone else does. And believe you me, if that boy comes prowlin' around you again, I'll be loaded for bear."

Matt rested his forearms on his thighs and leaned forward. "I'm assuming you've had previous contact with Alex Townsend?" He raised a brow and Hank nodded.

"Hank was there the other day when Alex approached me. He ran him off for me." Erin grasped the older man's hand and held it between both of hers.

"Kiddo, you know I'm never going to allow anyone to hurt you. I knew that boy was trouble waiting to happen when you first started seeing him all those years ago." Hank reached over and wiped a tear off her cheek. "But you were at that age when you were going to do what you wanted, not about to take advice from your parents or some dusty old cowboy." He shrugged. "When he went to prison, I figured he'd be back someday, and I've been ready for ten years. So don't be crying on my account."

"Would you like to stay at the Montgomerys' ranch until this problem is solved?" Matt smiled at Hank. "I think we can fit another air bed into Erin's bunkhouse."

"Or you could stay at the main bunkhouse, with the other hands," Erin suggested.

Hank shook his head. "I appreciate the offer, but I'm fine here. I'll just be more on my toes, now that I know that no-good bum is skulking around."

"Then let me at least install a security system here at your place." As the old-timer shook his head again, Matt continued. "Just a couple of cameras and an alarm. At least until we've taken care of this Alex business."

Hank stood. "I've done fine by myself for this long. Figure I can last until that little thug is gone for good. However the good Lord might choose to make that happen."

Matt and Erin stood when Hank shuffled toward the front door.

Matt shook his hand. "If you change your mind, let me know."

"You kids stop worrying about me. And, Matt, you focus on keeping my kiddo here safe, all right?"

"Will do." Matt paused as he and Erin walked down the porch steps. "The gate, barn and bunkhouse lock codes are being rekeyed tonight. I'll text you the new one as soon as I know it."

Hank gave him a thumbs-up before closing his front door.

On the way home, an oncoming car's headlights washed through the truck cab and Matt glanced at Erin. With her brows knit into a frown and her skin pale in the unnatural light, she resembled a frightened child. He had seen her mad, seen her laugh, seen her determined. But tonight was the first time he'd seen her scared.

His eyes back on the road, he asked, "Do you think you can talk him into the security system?"

"I doubt it. We could install some cameras and ask for forgiveness instead of permission. But I don't think he'd use an alarm. They take a while to get used to, and in the meantime he'd either be setting off false alarms or just not setting it."

"I get it." Matt's job was to protect Erin, not her ranch hand. But if anything happened to Hank, it would destroy Erin.

And somewhere deep in his gut, a suspicion stirred that *that* would destroy Matt.

Chapter Seven

The following afternoon, his empty stomach rumbling with embarrassing sounds, Matt held the door to Bo's Bar-B-Q Bonanza for Erin. The place was one big room with picnic tables and benches lined up in rows across the concrete floor. Erin led him to the back of a small line of people waiting to order at the counter.

"This might be the best smell I've inhaled since landing in Texas." Matt studied the menu on the wall, settling on a brisket sandwich with fries. He kept pace with Erin as they moved through the line, then handed the cashier his credit card. "I've got both of these trays."

Erin side-eyed him. "You don't have to buy me lunch."

"I know that."

"Then why—"

"Because I want to, okay?" Matt picked up his tray and headed to the drink station, where he filled a glass with iced tea.

"Thanks." Erin reached past him to grab a glass, playfully nudging his hip with hers. "I'm just used to paying my own way." Her voice didn't carry the same playful tone as her actions.

"I'm not sure using your parents' money is exactly paying your own way." It was a harsh thing to say, but

Erin lived in a bubble of advantages and seemed not to appreciate it.

Gathering silverware from containers on the drink station, Erin paused at his words and faced him. "I do have a trust set up by my mom's parents, but I won't have access to it until I'm older, and I have no idea what the contingencies will be. I receive a small monthly allowance from a trust my dad's parents set up for me. And when I say small, I mean it. The only other money I have to spend on myself now is what I make through riding lessons and dressage training. Maybe you shouldn't be so quick to judge when you don't know the facts." Erin strode across the room and sat at the end of one of the tables.

Ashamed of judging and embarrassing her, Matt hurried after Erin and took the seat across from her. "I'm sorry. You're right, I shouldn't have said that."

"I'm actually glad you did." With jerky movements, she unwrapped her silverware from the paper napkin rolled around it. "Otherwise, I might not have known what you thought about me." With the napkin covering her lap, she picked up her fork and stabbed at the food on her plate. "Or been able to straighten out your misconceptions."

Matt reached across and stilled her hand, holding it until she met his gaze. "I'm sorry for assuming something that's not true about you. It wasn't fair."

"I accept your apology." She pulled her hand from his. "But as for *fair*, look around. I'm still the black sheep of Winston after ten years." Erin scoffed.

Matt surveyed the room, noticing whispers aimed at Erin from other customers. "People around here really carry a grudge, huh?"

"Some of them have good reason to." She met Matt's gaze. "But I didn't expect so much animosity from you."

He fought against looking away from the hurt in her eyes. He'd caused that pain, and the least he could do was accept her silent reproach. "I really am sorry, Erin. I guess sometimes I'm quick to judge, and I have a tendency to say what I'm thinking."

"Forget about it. Let's just enjoy lunch." Her resigned smile didn't reach her eyes, a clear indication she'd not soon forget anything about his hurtful misconception.

When Erin finally focused on eating her food instead of stabbing it, Matt took a bite of his sandwich and changed the topic. "This is amazing. I definitely need to come back here and try the ribs."

With a forkful of pulled pork halfway to her mouth, Erin paused. "I hope you mean that."

"Why do you say that?" Matt tried for levity. "You hoping for another meal on me?"

But instead of smiling at his lame attempt at humor, Erin's expression darkened again. "Brandon and Lisa Bauer own this place. It's named after their son, Bo. He loved barbecue, and he loved the old cowboy TV show *Bonanza*."

Was. Loved. Past tense. A lump of sandwich seemed stuck in Matt's chest as he anticipated what she was about to say. He chugged some tea before Erin continued.

"Bo was their only child. He died from cancer when he was eight."

"So this restaurant is a sort of tribute to their son?" Matt asked.

Erin nodded. "They were already planning on opening a barbecue joint. Bo was super excited about it. But then they put it on hold when he was diagnosed. Later, they went forward with the plans, renaming it for Bo. Part of every dollar they earn goes to cancer research. And they hold benefits twice a year."

Impressed by the depth of Erin's caring about others, Matt made a mental note to not make any more ignorant assumptions about her. And especially not to voice them aloud.

Erin cleared her throat, this time giving him a genuine smile. "Anyway, back to our search."

They'd spent the morning visiting the places Matt had asked Erin to show him—the stolen goods' original hiding spot, and where the police had stopped her.

"How far from the roadblock was the charity you were supposed to return the van to?"

"Only a block away." She shook her head. "If I'd circled around the long way, in the direction Alex and Brad took, I probably would have missed the cops completely."

"Maybe so. But then who would you be today?" Matt arched a brow.

Erin's lips twisted to the side. "Not sure I want to consider the possibilities." Her expression fading, she shrugged. "Looking at it that way, I guess I'm lucky I got arrested."

"That's one of the toughest things about life. Learning lessons the hard way." Finishing his sandwich, Matt wiped the barbecue sauce from his fingers on a paper towel. "So, where to next?"

"The bar. We were supposed to all meet at Mom's."

"Your mom has a bar?" Matt couldn't picture the Southern society queen who'd hired him as a bar owner.

Erin laughed. "Mom's is a biker bar out on the southwest side of town. The guys all had bikes and hung out there, so they figured Sonny and the regulars would alibi us."

"Who's Sonny?"

"Mom's son."

"Of course he is."

"Mom owned the bar until she died. Sonny was always the bartender, and he became the owner after her death." Erin's words spilled out now. "That's where we need to go. See if any of the guys showed up that night."

"Hang on a minute." Matt massaged his temples, trying to slow down and think this through.

"Don't you see?" Her excitement grew. "If any of them did get there, they might have slipped up and said something."

"I don't feel comfortable walking into a biker bar without knowing the layout or anything else. Especially with you."

"What's the difference between Mom's and this place? You didn't have a problem walking in here without knowing anything about it."

"One potential difference could be a bunch of big bikers who don't like us asking questions on their turf."

"I used to go there all the time with Alex. I know Sonny. We'll be fine." Erin drained the last of her tea and stood. "Let's get going."

Matt sighed. It might not be the worst idea to check out Mom's. At least Erin wasn't just sitting around, scared of everything. She was being proactive, taking the bull by the horns, so to speak. But if it *was* the worst idea, it'd be too late to do anything about it by the time the door closed behind them.

Since Matt had offered to help her look for the loot, and especially since he'd agreed to go to the bar with her, Erin stayed in the truck until he went through his process of letting her out at Mom's.

As Matt took in the old, dilapidated building, Erin tried to see it as if it were her first time here. A faded wooden sign above the door that read *Mom's*. Neon beer signs in the two tinted windows, making it harder to see in than out. A long row of bikes in front of the bar, most of them backed in to make for an easier, quicker getaway.

Matt held the front door open for her, but stayed tight to her side as they entered. Erin's eyes took a long moment to adjust to the dim room, and when they did, every person in there was staring at them.

Erin faltered for a moment, then approached the bar with a big grin. "Hi, Sonny. It's been a while."

Sonny, a glass in one hand and a dish towel in the other, smiled at her, just as he always had in the old days. But back then, that smile had been almost pitying. Like she was in over her head, hanging out with Alex and his friends, and it was only a matter of time before she figured that out, too.

The burly man glanced at his watch. "About ten years, give or take. How you doin'?"

Shuffling of feet throughout the room, a few low comments between men at the tables, and Erin's memories of being a teenage rabble-rousing rebel evaporated, leaving behind images of a naive do-gooder who had fooled herself into thinking she could hang with the tough crowd.

"I'm good." She took a step back. "This is my friend Matt."

Both men nodded at each other, which apparently took the place of a handshake in situations like this.

Erin settled onto a barstool. "Can we get a couple of drafts?" While Sonny filled two mugs, Erin motioned for Matt to sit next to her instead of scanning the room like…well, like a bodyguard. "You hear Alex is back in town?" she asked the bartender.

Sonny glanced at her over the mugs as he set them in front of Erin and Matt. "A few of the guys mentioned seeing him. He hasn't been in here, though. Pretty sure having a beer with some of my clientele would violate his parole." He chuckled.

Erin took a long draw on her beer. "I know we were in here a lot, so you might not recall just one specific time, but do you remember if Alex, Brad, Kevin or Billy came in here the night of the *Charity Hold-up*?" Yes, their crime caper had an official name around town. "We were supposed to meet here afterward. I obviously didn't make it, but I was wondering if any of the guys did."

A man in biker leathers yelled from one of the tables. "You mean, did they stop in here for a quick beer while you were ratting them out to the cops?"

Brad Parker, Kevin Moore and Billy Jensen had been working at the charity for community service as part of their probation terms. But they'd been bikers long before that, and this bar had been their favorite haunt. Of course everyone in here hated her for snitching on their friends.

Her idea to come to Mom's for information seemed less and less like a good one.

Since the robbery, Erin had dealt with her guilt about stealing valuable items from her parents' guests, friends and neighbors. She'd sought redemption for being part of a caper that caused a man to have a stroke. Now she faced the flip side of the coin. She hadn't turned in Alex and the others to save herself from prison, although that's what most people thought. She did it because what they'd done was wrong. The moment Alex had pistol-whipped Liam O'Roarke, causing him to collapse, Erin knew she couldn't live with herself if she didn't report him. It was the same moment she'd realized what she thought was love was as nonexistent as Alex's *good* intentions.

But now she was seeing herself the way these men saw her—as a backstabber. A snitch.

She understood why they wouldn't want to help her. The code they lived by wasn't one of right and wrong, at least not in the sense of most people. It was based on loyalty to each other, regardless of what any of them had done.

Erin spun her barstool around and faced the room. "I'm sorry that you consider me to be the bad guy. But Alex put an innocent man in the hospital that night. And the police found out that he was my boyfriend before I even told them anything."

One of the men at the pool table walked toward her, slapping his cue against the palm of his hand. "Still doesn't make it right. Either you're loyal or you're a rat."

A chorus of *yeah, that's right, tell her* rose from various tables.

Matt stood and moved in front of Erin, and she finally understood how dangerous his job could be.

But before anyone made a move, Sonny wadded up his towel and threw it on the bar. "Y'all shut up and sit down. You're getting all worked up about something that happened years ago." He moved into the room, giving those still on their feet a hard look. "You think beating up on a woman is going to make bigger men of you?" His sneer as he went back behind the bar answered the question for them.

Matt sat again, rested his forearms on the bar top and angled himself toward Sonny. "Look, we didn't mean to cause any trouble. The thing is, Alex has been harassing Erin about the loot that disappeared back then. We thought if you could remember which of the guys made it to the rendezvous here that night, we might be able to help Alex find it and get him off Erin's back."

Sonny glanced at Erin, then back at Matt. But not before she caught a glimpse of the Sonny from the past. The one who had felt sorry for her.

Erin leaned in. "Which of them made it back here that night, Sonny?"

"Townsend, Parker and Moore. All of them except you and Jensen." He kept his voice low.

"Did they say anything? Or did you overhear them talking?" Matt asked.

Sonny's eyes slid to the bikers before he grabbed his towel off the counter. "All they knew was the cops showed up way faster than they'd expected. They hung out here for about an hour, knowing most of the guys here would give them an alibi. And when you—" Sonny looked at Erin again "—didn't show after an hour, they figured you'd been picked up. The other two kept whining about how you were going to turn them in, but Townsend told them he had you wrapped around his little finger and you'd never do that."

Erin swallowed back regrets that always skimmed the

surface of her emotions. Not regret for turning in Alex Townsend but regret for thinking he'd actually cared for her.

"The only reason I'm telling you this is because I never liked that guy," Sonny continued. "He was the new one in their group, but the other three acted like he could walk on water. Reminded me of those cult leaders you hear about on the news."

Matt nodded. "I'm aware of how easily some people fall under another's malicious spell."

Erin wondered for a moment if he meant her, or someone from his past. "Did they talk about the stolen stuff at all?"

Sonny shook his head. "They were trying to act natural. Didn't even get hinky about you until right before they left."

Matt leaned back when Sonny started wiping the bar in front of him. "Did you know about the robbery beforehand?"

"Me?" Sonny paused, his bar rag mid-swipe. "Nah. I don't think anybody did until the police set up the roadblocks and word started getting out. I figured out the part about them setting up their alibi here after overhearing what little I did."

"Thanks, man." Matt stood and shook Sonny's hand. "We appreciate your help."

"One last word of advice." Sonny leaned closer and kept his voice low. "When word got out about the loot disappearing, every lowlife in this county searched for it. That stuff ain't hidden around here, and it's a waste of time looking for it."

"Thanks again." Matt grabbed Erin's elbow before she could respond and steered her toward the door. And he didn't let go until she was seated in the truck with the door locked.

Mulling over what they'd learned, Erin waited for Matt to start driving before putting her thoughts into words. "So, where should we look this afternoon? The woods where they were first buried, maybe?" She watched the bikes grow smaller in the passenger-side mirror. "If you think about it, the fastest way to get rid of the loot would have been to move it somewhere close to the original hole."

Matt was silent for a mile marker, probably wondering why she was still so insistent on the loot being around here, even after Sonny mentioned the treasure-hunt riot that ensued after the arrests.

"It's clouding up." He craned his neck forward and looked up through the windshield. "And it'll be even darker in the woods. If you want to try for that area, I'd rather start early tomorrow morning."

Erin accepted his idea with a nod, thankful he didn't outright say that she was crazy to keep trying. She checked her watch. "In that case, I'd like to check in with Liam again. If that's okay with you."

"I thought you said you don't visit him this often."

"I usually don't. But I figure we'll be busy for the next several days, so this will be a good time to stop by."

"Next stop, Hidden Oaks."

Erin smiled as she watched the scenery pass by. It had been a good day so far, and nothing would spoil the rest of it.

Chapter Eight

Alex Townsend laughed as the truck he'd been following turned onto the road leading to the old folks' home. Erin had a surprise waiting for her there. Nothing gruesome. Just a little reminder that time wasn't on her side.

Twisting the throttle on his bar brother's bike, Alex continued straight on the main road, traveling like a bat out of hell. He preferred riding fast, especially after tailing Erin and her bodyguard boyfriend. That guy drove like Alex's grandmother used to—crawling along below the speed limit and slowing at every intersection. At least his grandmother had an excuse: she could barely reach the pedals and see through the windshield at the same time.

He couldn't understand why Erin didn't just hand over the loot and be done with it. She had to have it. Only thing that made any sense. Why she was dragging this out, pretending to search for it, was beyond him. But if she insisted, he'd keep having fun with her. At least, until Cowboy's deadline caught up with them.

The kid's marble in the oven had been perfect. And easy, too. Then all that running around to the kid's house and the old-timer's ranch. They'd been so upset, no one had noticed Alex. Hiding in the dark, but always one step ahead.

Unable to follow them into Mom's today, he'd called a friend inside the bar while he waited outside. He got the gist of why they were there. But it bothered him that Sonny had huddled with them at the bar. He might need to pay a visit to his favorite bartender and learn what the big secret was about.

But now, as he slowed to the town speed limit to avoid getting pulled over, full-visor helmet hiding his identity, he focused on his next plan to light a fire under dear *Eriss*. And it was a real humdinger, all right.

Chapter Nine

Matt noticed the receptionist's brows pulled into a worried frown when they approached the front desk. "I'm not sure how well your visit will go today. Liam is a bit frazzled."

Erin signed in and handed Matt the pen. "Why? What's happened?"

"He had another visitor a while ago, and after he left Liam seemed very upset. He's calmed down a little since then, but not much." The receptionist answered the ringing phone and placed the caller on hold. "We've notified Mrs. O'Roarke, and she's on her way. The police are already here."

"The police? What did this visitor do?" Erin pulled the sign-in sheet out from under Matt's hand before he could finish his signature. Skimming down the list, she tapped her finger on the name of Liam's last guest. *Alan*, followed by a squiggly line. "It has to be Alex. That's the same name he used last time he came here."

Replying to Erin's last question, the receptionist said, "Apparently, he threatened Liam. That's why we called the police."

"Who was on duty at this desk when the visitor checked in?" Matt turned the register sheet around and held it in front of her nose.

"Well, that would be… Let me just check the sign-in time—"

"Come on. We can deal with whoever screwed up later." Erin speed-walked through the maze of hallways to Liam's room.

The door stood open, and the small room seemed to overflow with people even before they stepped inside. Two policemen, an aide, a woman in a suit with a calm demeanor that practically screamed, *We are not responsible and you can't sue us*, and Liam, dressed in a somewhat fashionable sweat suit, sitting in his wheelchair, his hands in his lap, trembling.

"Liam!" Erin rushed across the room and crouched next to the elderly man. "Are you all right?"

As she laid her hand on his arm, he slowly lifted one of his to cover hers.

"What happened?" Erin spoke softly. "Who came to see you today?"

Liam's eyes closed. "When he was here the other day, he said his name was Alan and that you'd told him to come visit me." His voice fluttered like a newly hatched butterfly. "But today he told me he's Alex Townsend, the one who…" He opened his eyes, lifting his hand again to gesture to the room. "The one who put me in this place. I thought I recognized him the other day. Just couldn't think of the name."

Although he'd expected Liam's answer, Matt's pulse accelerated at the name of the man he was protecting Erin from. He stepped closer to the older gentleman, needing more information. "What exactly did he say to you today?"

One of the cops interrupted. "Just hold on here. Who are you two?"

Steve Folsom, the other officer and someone Erin knew well, answered. "She's a good friend of the victim."

"And I'm her bodyguard, protecting *her* from your suspect."

Pulling his eyes from Erin, Liam pinched his brow together as if trying to remember Alex's words. "He said if you don't give him all the stuff you stole, he was going to put me out of my misery."

"Liam…" Erin seemed at a loss for words.

"Threatening an old man in a wheelchair? That didn't upset me so much." He smiled wanly at Erin before turning back to Matt. "But when he said he'd pay a visit to my wife…" His voice broke, and he looked away, unable to hide the fear in his eyes.

Erin wrapped her arms around his shoulders. "It's okay. He's not going to hurt you *or* your wife. We'll make sure of that." She looked at Matt over Liam's head, her eyes holding as much desperation as Liam's did fear. "Right?"

No. Not desperation. Matt tried to sort the many thoughts running through his head. Hope. Erin was looking to him to help keep her hope alive. Hope that he'd be able to keep not only her but also Liam safe. Hope that he'd help ensure an end to Alex Townsend's evil machinations and threats.

But could he? He'd never felt the pressure of his job as much as he did in that moment. Oddly, most of the pressure stemmed from his heart.

Shaking off his doubts, he organized his thoughts.

His number one priority was Erin. But he'd call Nate about the O'Roarkes. His partner—no, boss—would agree they couldn't leave the older couple to the mercy of Townsend.

"Yes, of course." He managed a smile at both Erin and Liam. "We'll speak with Mrs. O'Roarke when she arrives and discuss security measures."

Erin's eyes softened, and the smile she returned his way did more to ease his doubts than all of Nate's pep talks combined.

After a few moments, Liam had calmed down enough to want a cup of coffee.

"You got it." Erin straightened out of her hug, brow raised at Matt. "You want one?"

Matt nodded. "I'll go with you so you don't have to balance three cups. I'm sure the police would like to finish taking Liam's statement."

It wasn't until they were several doors down the hall from Liam's room that Erin spoke. "I can't believe Alex threatened a sick old man. As if Liam has anything to do with me finding the jewelry."

"I'm sure it's meant as added motivation for you." Matt tried to keep his tone level but felt as enraged as Erin sounded. Only truly vile people went after children and the elderly. "Probably thinks his threats to hurt the O'Roarkes will make you try even harder, and faster, to find the stuff. Remember the message with Tommy's marble."

Erin, mouth pressed in a flat, firm line, turned a corner and stepped into a small kitchenette.

"How many other people do you think he's running around trying to intimidate?" Matt asked.

Erin filled three paper cups with coffee from a large carafe. "Not that many, to be honest. My parents will be in Europe for at least another week, and I don't really have any close friends anymore. Liam and Hank are about the only people I spend any time with at all, other than those I give riding lessons to. And there haven't been any lessons since before Alex got out of prison, so I can't think of a way he could find out who they are. The only reason he found Tommy was because he followed us to the store."

Matt picked up two of the cups, leaving one for her to carry. "That's good." Good for potential people Alex could threaten, but sad that Erin had only an old man in a care facility and her ranch hand as friends.

A few minutes after they returned to Liam's room, Maeve O'Roarke arrived, quick to sit by her husband's side and take his hand in hers. "The front desk said a visitor upset you and I should come right away." She looked around at Erin and Matt. "Who was it? What's going on?"

The police and staff had left, so Erin took a deep breath, then repeated the whole story. "I'm so very sorry. I feel responsible for him coming back into your lives."

The older woman left her husband's side long enough to give Erin a hug. "Don't be ridiculous. You've more than made up for your small part in that…past incident." She glanced at Matt.

"This is Matt. He's not just a friend." Erin looked at Liam, her cheeks flushed from her previous fib. "He's my bodyguard. My parents insisted on hiring him when they heard Alex was back in town."

"I think we need protection for you too, my love," Liam said to his wife. "He's threatened both of us, and I don't want to take any chances that he'll show up at our house and hurt you."

"I'd be happy to call my boss, see if he has someone available," Matt offered.

Maeve gave him a firm nod. "Can you check with him

right now? I'd like to get this taken care of so Liam can stop worrying."

"If you'll excuse me a moment, I'll make a call to get the ball rolling." Matt fished his phone out of his pocket. "And afterward, I'll need to have another word with the facility's administration. I'm not too happy that after I informed the receptionist of the possible danger Alex represented and to be on the lookout for a man of his description, he was able to walk into a resident's room unchecked."

"Really?" Maeve's countenance darkened like a storm rolling in. "Well, we'll just see about that. With as much as this place is charging, along with the status of most of its residents, they should be able to keep every one of them safe from ill-intended visitors. I'll be right back, dear." She laid a kiss on her husband's forehead and steamed out of the room, Matt following to make his call.

After speaking with Nate to arrange a bodyguard for Maeve, and an hour-long meeting with the owner of the facility, the head administrator, the chief financial officer and the front desk receptionists, the agreement reached provided 24/7 protection outside Liam's door by Resolute Security, with the facility and the O'Roarkes splitting the fee.

And as much as the increased revenue for his future co-owned business was appreciated, it was the warm glow in Erin's eyes when she looked at him when they left for the ranch that revived his spirit.

ON THE WAY HOME, Matt glanced at Erin. Her satisfaction with the security arrangements for the O'Roarkes no longer had her glowing. "You okay?"

"I'm furious." She leaned back against the headrest. "Ten years later, and the first thing to make me this mad since Alex hit Liam has to do with Liam again."

Matt understood her frustration. "We'll make sure Liam and Maeve are safe. Don't worry."

"The thing is, I've always hated physical violence." Erin's hands, resting on her thighs, curled into fists. "But right now, I want to punch Alex Townsend all the way back to prison."

"I'm sure you do, especially since he's messing with people you care about."

"We need to find him." Erin drummed her fisted hands on her thighs. "Today. Right now."

"Aside from the fact that my job is to keep Alex away from you, we have no clue where he is. And even if we did, beating him up would only put you in jail, not him." Matt kept his voice even so as not to aggravate her even more.

Erin fumed the rest of the way back, jumping out of the truck the moment Matt parked it next to the barn. She strode toward the building.

Still trying not to add to her ire, Matt refrained from reprimanding her on not waiting until he opened her door. "Where are you going?"

Erin yanked open the barn door but stopped long enough to answer him. "I need to go for a ride. Blow off some steam. Clear my head."

Dread that had nothing to do with Alex Townsend punched Matt in the gut. "You know I have to go with you, right?"

"I'm aware. But if you can't keep up, I'm not stopping to wait for you."

Matt followed her inside, and as Erin saddled Shadow, he did the same with Blaze. Thankfully, by the time they were done, she seemed a bit less combustible.

"I'm impressed." Erin handed a pair of gloves to him before pulling on her own. "You remembered how to do it."

"I might've snuck a look or two at what you were doing, just to make sure." Proud of getting the hang of some of this horse stuff, Matt pulled on the leather gloves with polar fleece lining. At least his hands wouldn't freeze as the late afternoon temperature dropped.

They led the horses out of the barn, and Matt made sure the door lock clicked before they swung into their saddles. He kept up with Erin's trot along the ranch road, but when they reached a grassy meadow off to their right, she kicked her heels once, and Shadow took off at a gallop.

Matt watched her go, knowing he wasn't ready to match her speed and keep up with her. But he also knew she wasn't trying to lose him, so he kept his anger in check and trotted after her. As his backside banged against the saddle, Matt winced and shifted as best he could.

Although he could still see Erin, her unbraided hair flying behind her, the distance between them grew. As if sensing they needed to catch up, Blaze segued into a lope that helped Matt sit rather than bounce.

Normally unwilling to tolerate pushback against his rules from his clients, Matt had surprised himself with cutting Erin some slack for this ride. It had been a roller coaster of a day, and as she herself had told him, Alex wouldn't hurt her as long as he thought she'd find the jewelry for him. Maybe her willfulness with him served as a counterbalance for her deference to almost everyone else in her life.

Blaze snorted.

Breaking out of his reverie, Matt gazed across the meadow. Tall grass, wildflowers, trees here and there. But no Erin. A jolt of panic kicked him in the chest. He let out on the reins, but white-knuckled the section he held, and let his horse do what she'd wanted to do all along. Gallop.

He had to trust that the horse knew its way across the property, because Matt's steering skills were limited to low-speed jaunts. But as they covered more ground, his fear of riding faded and he began to enjoy the ride. Almost the same exhilarating experience as riding a wave.

Matt leaned forward, his eyes watering from the cold air. A blurry shape materialized up ahead and transformed into Erin as he gained ground. She must have heard him, because she looked over her shoulder and reined in Shadow to a stop.

Blaze's primary goal must have been to catch up, because she slowed on her own and stopped next to Erin.

"Well, look at you." Erin arched a brow as Matt's horse circled around and nuzzled hers. "You galloped."

"I did." Matt gasped for breath. "But it's a good thing she stopped, 'cause I have no idea where the brakes are on this thing."

A faint smile curved her lips.

"I get it now. How it pulls the tension and stress from your body and frees your mind."

Erin nodded. "It's the only thing that does it for me."

"It's the same with surfing. Slide into the pocket of a

barrel wave or catch a point break, and it's just me and the wave."

Erin climbed down from Shadow, walked her to a tree and draped the reins around a branch. "You'll have to explain all those surfing terms to me one of these days."

"Happy to." Matt got off his horse and tied her next to Erin's. "Did the—" he turned to find her pacing in circles, her hands curling into fists and then opening, again and again "—ride help?"

"Yes, but that's the thing. When the ride's over, everything you're running from catches up with you again and fills your head and your heart and your soul." Erin massaged the back of her neck. "My entire body is like one big knot, and I just can't relax."

"I know that feeling, and I've got the perfect way to help you blow off some steam."

Erin froze mid-pace at her bodyguard's words. "What could I possibly do out here that would calm my anger?"

Matt raised his gloved hands in a defensive position. "You've been wanting to punch someone, so come on. Hit me."

Erin took a beat to stare at Matt in confusion. "What on earth are you talking about?"

"Trust me." Matt demonstrated what he meant by punching his right fist into his left palm. "This will make you feel better. There's nothing like pummeling a boxing bag to release all that negative energy. We don't have a bag, so use me."

Erin tilted her head to one side and considered Matt as an opponent. She'd never hit anyone in her life. "I don't know…"

"Just try it." Matt widened his stance.

With nothing to lose, Erin approached him. Her gloves were a far cry from what boxers wore, but at least they offered her knuckles some protection. She balled her hands into fists, raised them and—

"Put your thumbs on the outside of your fists. Otherwise, you'll break them."

After a quick adjustment of her fingers, Erin pulled back her right arm and drove her fist into Matt's palm with all the force of a gnat landing on an overripe banana.

"Seriously?" Matt scoffed. "I know you're packing a harder punch than that. *Hit* me."

"Fine. I'll *hit* you." This time she slammed her fist into his hand, satisfied when she felt him bracing for impact. "Happy?"

"Ecstatic." Matt reset his stance. "Now this time, say what you're upset about when you punch me."

With her lips twisted to one side, Erin imagined the cause of most of her torment. "Alex Townsend." *Punch.*

"Be specific," Matt demanded. "Why him?"

Saying his name aloud lit a fire in her veins, and she answered Matt with loud conviction. "For screwing up my life." *Punch.* "Twice!" *Punch. Punch.* "For Liam." *Punch.* "And threatening everyone I care about." *Punch.*

"What else are you mad about?"

Erin's answer came as swiftly as her punches. "My mother."

"Why?"

"For holding me hostage." *Punch.* "Controlling me." *Punch. Punch.* She alternated blows with her right and left hands. The crisp air chilled her cheeks, and she realized they were wet.

Not possible. She never cried.

"For hiring a bodyguard without even discussing it with me." The punches came fast and furious now. "And I have no privacy. You invaded my house. Put up cameras. Don't let me out of your sight."

Though she'd aimed the last words at him, Matt's tone never became defensive. "Who else?"

As her tears flowed, Matt blurred into an indistinct shape.

"Me."

At that, Matt's expression faltered.

As did her punches.

"I'm mad that I let Alex ruin my life. That I played a part in Liam's injuries. That I don't have the backbone to go against my mother or to start my own therapy ranch." Erin's fists fell to her sides, her ragged breaths disintegrating into sobs.

Matt wrapped his arms around her, his punching-bag hands holding her close.

Physically exhausted, mentally drained, Erin rested her cheek against his chest.

"Feel better?"

Although he kept his arms around her, Matt loosened his hug as Erin lifted her head and looked up into his eyes.

The silent moment held as Erin slid her arms around Matt's neck and kissed him. Probably breaking another one of his rules, but she didn't intend to break it alone. She kept her lips pressed against his until he kissed her back with a passion that chased away her demons.

At least, for now.

Chapter Ten

Matt sat on the front porch steps with his hands wrapped around a steaming cup of coffee, watching Erin work with the dressage horse in the corral. His momentary panic from waking up and finding her gone for the third day in a row had eased when he checked the security cameras and saw her in the barn with Hank.

His first instinct, anger at her not following his rules, had faded as he backed up the footage and reviewed it. She'd taken the same precautions before leaving the house that she had yesterday. And to be honest, he appreciated the extra shut-eye. Sleep had been a long time coming as he tried to make sense of what happened last night. Although Erin had initiated it, he never should have kissed her back, regardless of how much he'd enjoyed it. But he'd been ambushed by the sudden desire that overtook him when her sweet tongue slipped between his lips and the length of her body pressed against his.

I made a mistake. It won't happen again.

A tone from his phone alerted Matt to the front gate opening. He jumped to his feet, unzipped his jacket for easier access to his gun and rounded the bunkhouse. A truck made its way around the main house and continued toward them.

About to race to the corral and get Erin inside, a text chirped on Matt's phone. A quick glance showed Nate's name.

Don't get your panties in a bunch. It's just me.

"What is it?" Erin called to him.

Matt headed toward the barn's parking area. "Nothing to worry about. My boss is paying us a visit."

Leaning against the barn, Matt waited for Nate to climb out of his truck. "A heads-up would have been nice *before* you came through the gate."

"What would be the fun in that?" Nate grinned. "Figured a mini readiness test couldn't hurt."

"Your sense of humor could use some work." He led Nate toward the bunkhouse. "Seriously, what are you doing out here?"

"I want to go over the logistics of our new clients." Nate waited for a response before knitting his brows. "The O'Roarkes?"

"Oh, yeah. Man, that seems like it was weeks ago instead of just yesterday."

Nate pulled the collar of his jacket up. "I don't suppose you have any coffee."

"Coffee's the first thing that happens around here. Come on, I'll introduce you to Erin on the way."

They shifted their direction and walked down to the corral, where Erin waited inside the gate.

"Erin Montgomery, Nate Reed."

Nate reached across the fence to shake her hand. "Nice to meet you, Erin. I trust Matt's been taking good care of you?"

"I guess if I have to have a bodyguard, he's not too bad." She glanced at Matt. "He's come in handy a time or two."

"Good to hear."

In an innocent voice, Erin asked, "Are you here to do a quality-control check?"

Nate snorted. "I've worked with Matt long enough to know he's the best there is. Well, second best, after me." He gave his friend a sly wink. "I just came by to review the additional security we're putting in place for the O'Roarkes."

"Thank you. I appreciate you taking care of them." Her expression darkened. "If Alex hurt Liam or his wife, I couldn't live with myself."

"We aim to make sure that doesn't happen," Nate said.

"It was a pleasure meeting you." Erin turned and walked Redemption toward the center of the corral.

Inside the bunkhouse, Matt poured Nate a fresh cup and refilled his own.

"What was with the weird mane on that horse?" Nate asked.

Happy to know something about horses that his friend didn't, Matt said, "It's how they fix them for dressage horses. Don't you know anything about elite horse competitions?"

"I see she's rubbing off on you. Let's hope the opposite's not true."

"Ha! She should be so lucky."

Nate's eyes scanned the bunkhouse. "So, this log cabin is where she lives?" Nate took a sip and swore. "Damn it, this is hot."

"Give it a minute and it won't be. I never thought Texas got this cold." Matt led his friend back out to the front porch. "And yes, this bunkhouse is where she lives. And me, too, for the duration."

"It's small."

"Tell me about it." Matt grimaced.

"How many bedrooms?"

Matt gave his friend a wry smile. "Two, of course. Which reminds me, I've got a receipt for an air bed to turn in." He added, "I'm in the junk room."

"How fitting." Nate laughed. "Just so you stay there. You don't need any more complications like you had in LA with Meryl Duncan, mixing business with pleasure."

"Hey, everything seemed great until she started getting serious." Matt shrugged. "It was never meant to last, anyway."

"Have things been going better between you and Erin since the first day?"

"Definitely. It's still a bit of a battle from time to time, but she's not as hostile as she was on day one." Matt's gaze drifted to Erin, directing the black horse in movements.

"Exactly how much better *are* things going?" Nate asked, pulling Matt's attention to his boss's raised brow. "It's hard to believe you could go from not wanting to even take this job to that wistful stare when you look at her in a matter of days."

"Wistful?" Matt scoffed. "Did Bishop give you one of his word-of-the-day calendars?"

Nate sipped his coffee, apparently waiting for a serious answer.

But Matt changed the subject. "Speaking of Bishop, has he had any luck tracking down Alex?"

"Not a trace." Nate had given the job of finding their nemesis to his brother-in-law and convenient office-next-door private investigator. "The guy hasn't met with his parole officer since he got out, and there's a warrant out for him on that. Not sure how his escapades at Hidden Oaks will factor into the whole situation." He paused. "I'm still waiting to hear why you look at Erin like a lovesick puppy."

"Give it a rest, Nate." Matt shrugged. "She's just not... who I thought she'd be. I admire her for trying to make up for her mistakes."

"Matt—"

"Chill, *boss*. I know you're just worried about the company's reputation if Mrs. Montgomery disapproves of us, but she won't. What happened with Meryl was a one-time thing. A job opportunity as her personal bodyguard that turned *personal* after I moved into her house." Matt side-eyed Nate. "But you have to admit, considering how things worked out for you and Sara, this feels like the pot is calling the kettle black."

Falling in love with Sara, the woman he'd been protecting in Resolute, was the reason Nate hadn't returned to their business in California.

"That's different. We'd known each other years earlier."

"Uh-huh."

"She was my sister's best friend. Practically part of the family."

"Uh-huh."

Nate blew out a breath.

"Don't worry. Nothing will ever happen between Erin and me." *And nothing* serious *will ever happen with anyone*. Matt's parents had shown him the worst-case scenario of a marriage—one that ended in tragedy. And most of the foster families he'd lived with hadn't been much better. They had all taught him well. He stuck to casual relationships and ended them as soon as they took a turn toward long term.

Although the passion of their kisses still lingered within him, Matt's determination to avoid getting too close to anyone stayed resolute. And especially with Erin. Because it would be unprofessional. It would jeopardize a renewed partnership with Nate. It would mean he believed she deserved her second chance. And giving someone a second chance could kill you.

"Glad to hear it," Nate said. "Now let's go over the plan for keeping the O'Roarkes alive."

Matt shook off old memories best forgotten. "Finally. I thought you'd never get to it."

"I'm assigning Charlie to Mrs. O'Roarke. She'll be with her 24/7, like you are with Erin."

"What about Liam?" Matt asked.

"Hidden Oaks has a contract with a security agency. They agreed to post one of their men outside Liam's door until this is resolved. Hidden Oaks decided to pick up the full bill since we're not providing the man, and because they don't want the O'Roarkes to sue them."

"That's good news."

"Liam and his wife wanted one of our men instead, but I don't have anyone else available." Nate stretched his legs out to a lower step. "I assured them the other company has an excellent reputation. They don't provide bodyguards, just big men with bigger muscles who guard doors. And they do it well."

"That will make Erin happy." Matt focused on his coffee mug to avoid looking at her. He didn't need another round of Nate's unsolicited and unnecessary advice.

"So, you've obviously kept our client safe. Any updates for me?"

After Matt gave his boss a rundown of the week's activities so far, Nate let out a low whistle. "You've been busy."

"Yep. And as soon as Erin's done working with the horse, we'll head out to look for the stolen goods again. We've got more precise information on where the police searched during the original investigation. We're going to move beyond that perimeter."

"Is it wise to take Erin out on these searches? It seems like a risk."

"Alex Townsend won't bother her because he wants what we might potentially find. And unless the police find and arrest him for parole violations, this will never end. If we locate and turn in the loot, he has no leverage over her."

Nate tipped his head back and looked toward the sky with his well-known thinking look. "He might want to take revenge if she foils his plans."

"Look, the day after I arrived, Erin tried to sneak out to search. Agreeing to help her was the only way I could get her to stop doing that." Matt chuckled. "Short of handcuffing her to something sturdy in the house. But if I have any reservations, I'll end the searches. If things get that dangerous, I know she'll sit tight inside."

"What makes you so sure?"

"Because she agreed to my rules." *Sort of.* "And rule number one is to stay near me and do what I say."

"Let's hope it doesn't come to that level of danger." Nate stood. "Keep in touch with Charlie, okay? If either of you run into trouble, y'all can back each other up faster than anyone else can get here from Resolute."

"Will do, but I doubt it'll be necessary." Matt walked Nate back toward his truck. "Erin and I will be just fine."

"We know the police already searched here." Impatience filled Matt's voice.

Erin looked up at him. "Why are you so grumpy?"

After Nate left, he and Erin had gone over their printed maps one more time before beginning their search where the jewelry had originally been buried. With their heads together, shoulders touching, fingers brushing, when Erin had gazed into his eyes with the same passionate fire as the previous evening, it took all of his willpower to not take her in his arms and kiss her again. He couldn't, because he'd already decided their first kiss was a mistake. And he'd assured Nate nothing was going on. Which was why he was grumpy.

"I'm not grumpy."

"I just want to look around here first before we move farther out." Erin crouched next to an oak tree and sifted the detritus at its base through her fingers. "Five more minutes. That's all I ask." Erin crab-walked to another tree and dragged handfuls of dirt and decomposed leaves away from its trunk.

"We're wasting time." Matt compared the police report map on his phone with the area. "The perimeter of the original search is another fifteen feet out from here."

Erin looked up at him. "You shouldn't be so eager to give up. You do know there's a reward for finding the jewelry, don't you? And if *we* find it, *you* get the reward."

He remembered Nate mentioning a reward. But that wasn't why he was there. "You're the one who's searching. I'm just along to keep you alive."

"You say that now. But wait until they hand you that big old check." She looked up at him and winked before digging her hands deep into the mulch again. "Ouch!"

"What happened?" Despite his frustration with her a moment ago, Matt raced to her side.

"Not sure." She brushed dirt off her hand and inspected it. "Something bit me, or maybe I cut my finger."

Matt took her hand in his and examined it. "Looks like a puncture. Could it have been a poisonous snake?"

Erin scoffed. "Unless the snake only had one fang, I'm pretty sure I'm safe on that account."

"We still need to see what it was." Digging through the handful of leaves she'd dropped, Matt added, "I'll have to get you to the emergency room if it was a bug carrying a virus. Ticks carry Lyme disease, right?"

As she poured water on her hand from her bottle, Erin scoffed. "You really are a city boy, aren't you? Ticks don't bite and go on their merry way. They latch on and don't let go."

"Still... Wait a minute." He twisted his fingers in the crumbled leaves and lifted them, holding a mud-encrusted earring toward her.

A ray of sun sparkled through part of the earring, and Erin took it from him. "This stone is an emerald."

"How can you tell it's real?"

"I've seen enough of them, I *own* enough of them, to recognize one." Erin turned it every which way. "I guess it could be a fake, but you can tell the setting is genuine gold because it's not tarnished." Her face lit up. "See? The loot is still here. Somewhere."

Matt dreaded ruining her hopes—trusting her gut and being right must rate almost as high as finding the piece of stolen jewelry. But for all they knew, this could be dime-store costume jewelry. "Let's not get too excited until we check the earring against the list of stolen items in the police report."

"Don't be such a Donnie Downer." Erin ran back to the truck and grabbed her folding spade. Returning to the tree where they'd found the earring, she dropped to her knees and dug.

Matt frowned as he watched her. "It just dawned on me, shovels are useless. Whoever took the jewelry wouldn't have had time to bury it again here before the cops arrived."

Erin paused, both hands on the spade. "I'm an idiot." Standing, she brushed dirt off her jeans. "I should have thought of that."

"Then I'm an idiot, too. Don't be so hard on yourself."

With slumped shoulders, Erin trudged back to the truck and put her folding shovel in the bed.

Matt berated himself. To him, searching for the loot was a lost cause. But for Erin, it was a way to own her previous actions and try to make up for them. He couldn't stand seeing her so defeated. And he *had* promised to help her.

"All he could have done was hide it somewhere no one would look," Matt said. "He must have planned on coming back later and getting it, but either he got arrested or left town."

"So we need to figure out the routes they each took after they left the woods and check along them." She straightened, her voice filling with enthusiasm. "Come on. There's enough daylight to start looking for hiding places before we call it quits for the day."

After mapping out routes for each accomplice from the earring's location to Mom's bar, Matt drove along the most likely one that Kevin took. It cut across the state road on a diagonal, connecting directly with another side road. "Where do these smaller roads lead to?"

"Other wooded areas, houses here and there for people who like their privacy, a ravine, an abandoned mine and a lot of old abandoned houses. Ramshackle messes, mostly. But some people own seasonal cabins, either for hunting or just a break from the city."

"People who like their privacy," Matt repeated. "Like reclusive millionaires?"

Erin sputtered a laugh. "More like reclusive meth cookers. Sheriff Reed and her department bust them from time to time, but new ones always spring up." She turned toward him. "We don't want to go searching anywhere near them."

"What if Kevin gave a meth-cooking friend the loot to hold for him?"

"Then it's gone for good. Either in an explosion and fire or pawned for more cooking supplies." Erin grimaced. "Either way, whoever he gave it to would be dead by now. Most cookers don't last ten years."

Matt continued driving the route, for now ignoring the even smaller roads branching off. "I'm curious about something you mentioned yesterday."

"What did I say?"

"Something about wanting to start your own therapy ranch." He glanced at her lips, curving into a smile. "You mean like what you're doing with Redemption? Working with injured horses?"

Erin shifted in her seat, turning toward Matt as much

as the shoulder harness would allow. "No. An equine therapy ranch works with people who are dealing with physical injuries or emotional trauma. Mental illness sometimes, too."

"I don't understand—who does the therapy? The horses?"

She laughed. "In a way. I'm not a licensed therapist, so I'd hire at least one, maybe more." Erin grew more animated the longer she talked. "They would work with the clients in conjunction with the horses. Someone may just want to pet or brush a horse. Someone else might want to ride. I knew a guy in college, a paraplegic, who learned to ride after his accident. It helped him regain a sense of control in his life."

Matt's opinion of his client rose once again. Despite his assurances to Nate, as well as his pledge to himself to not get involved, something about Erin drew him in. His interest in her was going beyond a professional need to keep her safe. "What got you interested in that?"

"I've worked with horses my whole life. But after the burglary, I had a lot of anxiety and I realized that being around them, even just grooming Shadow and Blaze, calmed me." Her voice took on a pensive tone. "I already knew about equine therapy, and that was when I first considered getting involved with it. I figured if the horses had that much of an effect on me, they could help others who had even bigger issues. It can help people learn to communicate, cultivate trust, and so much more. I wanted everyone who needed it to experience it. So I learned everything I could about it."

Turning onto a road Erin indicated, Matt said, "Sounds like a big undertaking."

"It is, but it'll be worth it. I'm hoping Mom will let me

tap into the trust her parents set up for me. Technically, I can't touch it until I turn thirty. But this may qualify for an exception. Regardless of the trust, the ranch will be a nonprofit. I'll have to depend on donations, grants and fundraising events for revenue."

"Maybe your parents can host one for you."

Erin snorted. "I won't hold my breath, but you never know."

He glanced over and caught her watching him. "What?"

"Just wondering what the dream is for you. Got any particular life ambitions?"

It wasn't that Matt wanted to keep his goal a secret from Erin. He rarely spoke to anyone about stuff like that. Nate, once in a while. Between a father who would ridicule and beat him, a mother who had her own life to worry about and several foster brothers and sisters who used information to gain favor, he'd learned to keep his cards close to the vest. But Erin had shared her plans with him.

"Nate and I were partners in our security company in California. My goal now is to buy into Resolute Security as a fifty-fifty owner. He had started the company before I moved to Texas, but from the moment I arrived, resurrecting our partnership has been the plan."

"So you're already doing what makes you happy?" Erin asked.

Matt nodded. "I enjoy it, and I'm good at it."

"It must be nice to have found your passion at a young age." Her tone seemed almost envious as she looked through the side window and pointed to what looked like a dirt parking lot.

He pulled into the lot and stopped the truck. "What is this?"

"People who hike this area leave their vehicles here. The ravine's a little way beyond it." Erin reached for her door handle, then rolled her eyes when he shot her a look. "I'm getting out, so if you insist on doing your bodyguard thing, you best hurry."

Blocking her door seemed pointless out there unless Alex was playing sniper, but Matt figured reinforcing the rules couldn't hurt. There could come a time when his rules defined the line between life and death for Erin.

She led the way through trees, shrubbery and rocks until they came to the edge of the ravine. "See the piles of boulders along the ravine floor? There are crevices between the rocks that create perfect hiding places."

"Worth checking out, I guess. But how do we get down to the bottom?"

"There's a trail that leads down. Like I said, people hike through here. Usually when the weather is better, but not having an audience while we search is probably a good thing."

"Drop a pin here on the map." Matt glanced at his watch. "Let's head home, and we'll come back tomorrow."

Between the icy breeze and her huge grin, Erin's face glowed. Although the ravine seemed like another long shot, Matt crossed his fingers that they'd find the loot here. It would bolster her confidence in this decision, and maybe others she'd make in the future.

Tomorrow would tell.

Chapter Eleven

Saturday morning, Matt parked in the area near the ravine where they had stopped the day before but left his truck idling for heat. Leaning forward, he looked up through his windshield at the dark, threatening clouds gathering above them. It snowed in the California mountains, but this damp, frigid weather in southern Texas blew his mind.

"Looks like rain." Erin tugged on gloves.

With his weather app open on his phone, Matt disagreed. "Says it might sprinkle a little, that's all. Heavier rain possible later in the week."

"Well, let's get to gettin', then." Erin waited until Matt turned off the truck, then picked up her backpack and climbed out without waiting for him to open her door.

"Hey, you know—"

"Yes." Layered in clothes, Erin hunched down inside her barn coat. "I know we're the only two people dumb enough to be out here in this weather."

Matt followed her since she knew the way to the trail that led down. The ravine, not too wide but deep, stretched out in front of them until it curved out of sight.

"This is what I'm talking about." Erin approached a grouping of boulders. "These crevices where the rocks meet make perfect hiding places. If Kevin shoved the bag in far enough, no one hiking past would even see it."

"*If* Kevin took the stuff." Matt scanned the floor of the gully, discouraged by the number of rock piles. "And *if* he hid it here." He moved to a nearby pile and reached into a crevice.

"Check for snakes first."

Matt yanked his arm out. "You couldn't mention that sooner?"

"I keep forgetting you're not much of an outdoorsy nature guy," Erin said.

"I thrive outdoors. But Texas is a far cry from California."

"Well, you live in Texas now. Maybe read a book about your new home." Erin glanced at him with a straight face. "At least learn about all the ways you can die here, so you can avoid them."

Matt's huff of exasperation formed a cloud in front of his face. "Are you going to tell me how to check for snakes?"

"Find one of these lying around. Make sure it's strong enough that it won't break." Erin raised her arm and waved a long, sturdy stick in the air. "If you see a snakeskin without a snake, there's a good chance he's in there somewhere."

As he looked for a stick amid the piles of wood debris on the floor of the ravine, Erin added, "They like to hide in the wood, too."

Regretting his decision to help her search this area for the loot, Matt picked up a stick with care, tested it to confirm its sturdiness and began poking into crevices.

While they worked their way down the ravine, the

sky darkened even more, and Erin pulled her knit beanie down over her ears. "Looks like some rain is moving in."

"The weather forecast this morning said a chance of showers farther north, but we shouldn't have any problems around here." Matt fished his phone from his pocket and opened the weather app. "And this still says just a chance of sprinkles."

Erin raised a brow. "If you believe the weather forecasters in Texas, I've got some swampland to sell you."

They continued the search for the stolen jewelry until lightning streaked the sky and thunder bellowed a few seconds later. Matt bent his head back to look up, blinking against fat drops of rain that splatted against his face.

Erin—one; forecasters—zero.

"We should go home and wait for the storm to clear, then come back." Erin turned around, toward the way they'd come.

"We've already come this far. I'd rather finish this area today and be done with it." Matt wiped his face. "Let's give it a few more minutes. Worst-case scenario, we get wet."

Erin shook her head. "Worst-case scenario, we drown."

"What are you talking about?" Matt asked. "It's just a little rain."

"You ever hear of a gully washer? It's a storm in a ravine that can cause a flood. And we've had so much rain lately, the ground is already saturated."

Matt shrugged. California sometimes had flash floods in the desert, and along the coast mudslides took houses over the edge of cliffs. But this ravine seemed safe. "Let's just make it down to that curve. Then we'll take a break and go back to the truck."

"Matt, you know a gully is a ravine formed by water flow, right? Like the one we're standing in?" Erin shouted over the rain that had become a downpour. "We need to get out of here."

With the conditions worsening by the moment, Matt didn't argue. He'd been searching close to one wall of the ravine and turned to head back to the trail. But he waited for Erin, several paces behind now and working her way toward him from the center of the gully.

"Do you need help?" Matt yelled to her. He took one step in her direction before water surged over the edge of the ravine in every natural depression. Cascading down and filling the gully floor, it raced toward them. Matt's heart stopped and he could barely breathe as he lunged toward Erin with his hand outstretched.

Erin glanced at the flash flood, back at Matt, her eyes wide with terror. She reached for his hand. Their fingers touched.

The narrow ravine forced the flash flood into a wall of water bearing down on them.

Matt wrapped one arm around a boulder and grabbed Erin's hand with the other. But his strength couldn't match that of Mother Nature.

"Erin!" Matt's bellow evaporated within the roar of the flood as Erin disappeared into its depths.

ERIN'S EYES OPENED. She lay flat on the ground, Matt leaning over her. "You're alive." Her voice, raw and relieved, faltered. "Or am I dead?"

His smile tentative, Matt said, "We're both alive."

"But how—"

"I was behind you the whole way. It took a few minutes to work my way to your tree, but with my weight on it, too, it snapped. The water swept us here to the mouth, and I managed to get us up on the bank." He glanced at the violent sky. "Right now, we need to find shelter." Taking hold of her arms, Matt pulled her into a sitting position.

Her howl of pain froze him on the spot.

"My...shoulder." She gasped, tears stinging her eyes as she got to her feet unassisted. "I think it's dislocated."

"Let me take a look." With gentle fingers, Matt probed her left shoulder and disagreed with her diagnosis. "Definitely subluxated, but not fully dislocated. I can pop it back in."

"Oh, no you can't." Erin wasn't about to chance permanent damage to her arm by trusting her bodyguard's diagnosis and battlefield remedy.

The steady look in his eyes calmed her even as he took hold of her arm. "Our security training included first aid. I've done this before." He pulled it straight, then eased the ball back into the joint before she realized what he was doing.

After another gasp of pain, Erin smiled with relief. "I take it back. You *can* fix it." She lifted her arm in amazement. Sore, but mobile.

"Be careful with it. Once it gets subluxated, it's easier for it to pop out again." Matt scanned the area. "I'm sure the parking area is a mudflat by now. You have any ideas for shelter around here?"

Erin looked around, trying to get her bearings. "I've seen a few hunting cabins not too far east of here when I've been out riding."

Matt took hold of her uninjured hand and they battled

against wind gusts and sheets of rain, this time searching for protection from the elements.

Erin stumbled toward the vacant cabin, Matt's arm around her waist to support her. "Check under everything on the front porch. There's a good chance they hid a key somewhere." Her body shivered against the cold.

Matt found the promised key inside a faded garden gnome. "Got it." He shepherded Erin inside, then shut and locked the door behind them.

"I can't believe we survived that." Erin's voice trembled as she realized how close to death she'd come.

Wrapping his arms around her, Matt pulled her into his embrace. His steady heartbeat drummed against her, calming her frenzied pulse. "You're safe now." His reassuring words soothed her even more.

The shock of nearly drowning still knotted her stomach, but in his arms she found momentary peace.

"I'll keep you safe, Erin," he whispered into her ear.

She heard the sincerity in his words. And the way he held her made her feel she was the only thing that mattered to him.

But the cold still lingered under their soaked clothes in the frigid cabin. Matt pulled her even closer, careful of her sore arm. "We need to get you warm."

She'd never felt more vulnerable—or more safe—than at this moment. As the storm raged outside, Erin recognized the subtle shift between them as Matt moved her near the fireplace.

"Sit here. I'll find some blankets and, hopefully, some dry clothes for you." He glanced around the small, rustic cabin. "But first, I'll get a fire started with these." He moved to a pile of dry logs in a corner, next to a bundle of kindling and a container of matches.

Erin sank down by the hearth, desperate for the warmth she hoped would come. At least the cabin was dry, offering refuge from the unrelenting rain that drummed against the roof.

Kneeling by the stone fireplace, Matt arranged the wood. With the strike of a match, flames flared in the kindling and reached up to the tented logs above it. As the fire grew, its bright glow chased away some shadows, creating an unexpected coziness.

Matt glanced at Erin, still shivering, and disappeared into another room. When he returned, he carried a pile of blankets and quilts. "You need to get out of those wet clothes," he said, his voice gentle but firm.

She hesitated, her eyes dropping. "Just give me a blanket and some privacy," she murmured, her voice barely audible over the now-crackling fire. After Matt helped her shrug off her coat, Erin's fingers fumbled at the buttons of her shirt. But they were too numb with cold to cooperate.

Kneeling in front of her, Matt reached out and stilled her hands. "Let me help." He kept his eyes on hers as he worked the buttons free. The shirt slid off her shoulders and she drew in a sharp breath as the cold air hit her skin. Matt grabbed a thick quilt from the pile and wrapped it around her. "This will help."

Erin pulled it tighter, grateful for its warmth, before she stood and toed off her soggy boots. Matt helped unfasten her jeans, then she turned away from him and peeled everything else off within the privacy of her quilt cocoon.

Back in her seat by the fire, where Matt had already spread several blankets to make a pallet, she watched him take off his own soaked jacket and shirt. The fire's glow highlighted lingering drops of rain on his chest and cast shadows that defined his muscles' sharp lines and angles.

When he caught her looking and gave her a faint smile, heat blazed in her cheeks, and she looked away. Wrapped in another of the blankets, he sat next to her, his body close but not touching. "Lean against me. Shared warmth will help."

Erin's instinct was to refuse, to continue to grasp for her elusive independence, but she was too cold to argue. She shifted closer and rested against him. He rubbed his hand up and down her uninjured arm, attempting to chase away the lingering chill.

As the fire grew warmer, Erin relaxed for the first time since the water had dragged her under. Her head leaned against Matt's shoulder, and she closed her eyes.

"Thank you," she whispered.

Matt's arm tightened around her. "Always."

As the comfortable silence between them grew, Erin lifted her head. Her eyes met his, and for a moment neither of them moved. He stared at her openly, his gaze moving over her face as if to commit every detail to memory. Her pulse quickened again, this time not from fear but from the undeniable pull between them.

"You know, you're not just someone I protect." Matt spoke in a low voice, rough with emotion. Almost as if the words cost him something to say. His hand moved from her arm to her face, his thumb brushing against her cheek. "You're much, much more."

His eyes searched hers as his words set her world spinning.

Moving with care, Matt closed the distance between

them, brushing her lips with his. A question more than a demand.

Erin's breath caught, and everything slowed down. Pressing her mouth harder against his, her fingers tangling in his damp hair, she gave him an answer he couldn't misinterpret. The kiss deepened, shifting from hopeful to desperate.

The blanket slipped from Erin's shoulders, and Matt drew her closer, his hands sliding down her back as she responded by tracing the planes of his chest with her fingers.

"Are you sure?" he murmured against her lips.

She pulled back and met his gaze. "Yes." And while her heart agreed, the voice in her head threw up roadblock after roadblock. *Is this the right decision?* But the desire within her banished the voice. "I want this."

Moving together, they shed the barriers between them just as they'd shed their wet clothes. Each passionate kiss, each tender touch, reinforced the trust they shared.

Matt's hands slid down to her waist, his firm touch guiding her to lie back, his body following hers in a seamless, natural motion. His lips trailed kisses from her mouth to her breasts and down, farther and farther. Erin arched into the warmth of his tongue, losing herself to his touches. Time and place disappeared as her release careened toward her and hurled her into an alternate dimension she hadn't known existed.

When Matt reached for his pants and pulled a condom from his pocket, Erin shook her head and switched positions with him. "My turn." She nipped at his earlobe, then let her lips wander, leaving a path of kisses along his jaw and across his chest, all while the crinkle of foil sounded nearby.

Her movements, unguarded and free of hesitation, were cut short of her goal when, seconds after Matt finished rolling the condom on, he wrapped his arms around her and turned until she lay beneath him once more.

With an achingly beautiful expression that she wanted to remember always, he whispered, "I can't wait."

Her shoulder pain a fading memory in the moment, Erin wrapped her hands around his shoulders, her legs around his back. "Yes."

Before she could take another breath, he thrust inside, and a silent scream pulled from her mouth.

Hands clutched at skin, then twisted in blankets as she soared higher than she'd thought possible with each subsequent movement.

And when they stilled, lying entwined and their breathing heavy, Erin rested her head on Matt's chest, noticing how the rhythm of his heartbeat matched her own.

Matt lifted his head just enough to look into her eyes. "You're beautiful."

Her breath caught. She'd been called beautiful before, but never with such awe, as though the word itself was inadequate.

"I don't—" she began.

But he silenced her with another kiss, one filled with an intensity that left no room for doubt.

She felt beautiful. And more importantly, for the first time in what seemed like forever, she felt whole.

She hadn't expected the emotions to hit her with such force. At first, it had only been the pull between them, especially after just escaping a watery death. But now it transcended that. She couldn't deny their connection.

But a moment later, that discouraging voice she'd banished earlier rallied.

I thought I could trust this decision, but now... I don't know.

Her mind went back to the struggles she'd had trusting herself, trusting him. Trusting anyone. She had felt safe in his arms. But now she wondered if these new feelings were real, or had she just fallen into old patterns, making decisions based on the need for someone to rely on?

Is it him I want? Or...just comfort?

She couldn't ignore what had just happened. But could she trust her own instincts? Wanting Matt frightened her, but she had to believe he was worth it.

This vulnerability exposed her in a way she hadn't expected. But it also made her realize something. It wasn't just about trusting him. It was about trusting herself. Her ability to navigate this whirlwind of emotions, to believe she could make the right decision for once, even if it wasn't the easiest one.

And maybe, just maybe, trusting him was the right decision.

MATT LAY IN the flickering firelight, Erin's warmth pressed against him. His heart still pounded in his chest, and though the physical release had been intense, the emotions seemed almost unbearable. He'd had no intention of developing personal feelings for her. But now that he'd crossed a line that he couldn't uncross, the possible consequences tormented him.

It hadn't been just the possibility of losing a client on

his watch that had tightened his chest with fear in the gully. It had been losing Erin. The rising waters had swept her away, shaking him to his core, and he'd discovered his feelings toward her were complicated. Different from those he should have for a client. Stronger than he experienced when attracted to a woman. His gut told him if he fell for Erin, it wouldn't be his usual casual fling, but instead a serious relationship.

And serious wasn't something he'd been looking for.

Matt's mind went to his training, to the number one rule he lived by—let nothing interfere with the job. But with Erin, things weren't that simple. She wasn't just his client anymore. She was the woman who had changed everything he thought he knew about self-control. About boundaries.

"I never thought I could trust anyone like I trust you," she whispered.

Matt's breath caught in his throat. Her words were like a thread pulling him further into her, into something he wasn't sure he was ready for. He had always kept women at arm's length—had always been the one to step back, to guard his heart, his feelings. But here, with her in his arms, he felt something shift within him. Something soft, something he hadn't realized he'd been craving.

His gaze drifted to Erin's face, a slight smile curving her lips. He brushed a strand of hair from her forehead, his fingers lingering a moment on her skin. The impulse to pull her closer was overwhelming.

I'll never be able to go back to being just her bodyguard after tonight.

Chapter Twelve

Alex Townsend crept from tree to tree on the Montgomerys' property, nearing the closed-up barn while avoiding the security cameras that bodyguard's lackey had installed. He snickered as he pictured Erin's face when she'd found the surprise he'd left in her oven.

But his amusement soon faded. The little boy's marble had been meant to light a fire under her search for the missing jewelry. And yet, Saturday morning had arrived and still no results.

Well, today she'd understand the consequences of her *in*actions.

Less than an hour earlier, Alex had watched Erin drive off with her hired protector, which meant only Hank, the over-the-hill cowboy who fancied himself a gunslinger, would be around.

The big black horse stood inside the corral, right where he'd seen it when he paid Erin a visit on Monday. And the corral was one area the security cameras didn't cover. Keeping an eye on the barn, he ran to the corral gate and let himself inside.

He'd never ridden but had always admired horses. Proud, powerful, majestic. And this one, as black as the devil himself, held him in awe.

It was a shame what he had to do to teach Erin a lesson. A damn shame.

Speaking in a soft, calm voice, he approached the horse with slow steps. When he got close enough, he grabbed hold of the halter so they stood side by side.

Then Alex reached with his other hand to the hunting knife on his belt.

He sensed the horse's nervous energy pulsating through the air and tightened his grip on the halter. The animal's dark eyes rolled and its hooves shuffled in the dusty corral, as if it understood Alex's intent.

As he raised the blade toward the horse's neck, something caught his eye. The barn door stood wide-open, and Hank headed toward the corral with two more horses.

"Stop right there!" Alex yelled.

"Alex!" Hank's shout cracked through the tension. The older man unsnapped the lead ropes and smacked the horses on their hindquarters, sending them in the opposite direction before he continued toward the corral gate with his revolver pointed straight at Alex. "Drop the knife and let the horse go. Now."

Alex sneered, tightening his hold. The horse jerked its head, testing his grip. "One step closer, old man, and I'll do it."

Hank froze for a heartbeat, his eyes narrowing. Alex saw the hesitation and knew he had the upper hand. Hank opened the corral gate wide and stepped inside, the revolver in his hand.

They circled each other, Alex holding tight to the horse's halter to keep it between them. The animal's panic grew, and its hooves churned the dirt.

"You're not walking out of here if you hurt that horse." Hank's voice was steady.

"Big talk from an old-timer who's too scared to pull the trigger." Alex barked a laugh, but he knew darn well if the horse went down, he'd be the fool who brought a knife to a gunfight. "What's it gonna be, Hank?"

Hank answered by firing a shot into the air. The loud crack shattered the standoff. The horse reared, its front hooves lashing at the air as it pulled free from Alex's grip. He stumbled back, and when the horse's hooves came down, it backed into Hank, knocking him to the ground. The revolver slid across the dirt and landed beyond his reach.

"Damn it!" Alex snarled, lunging to grab the halter again, but the horse fled through the open gate.

Hank scrambled to his knees, but Alex was on him in an instant. With a wild roar, he slammed into Hank, driving him back down. The older man grunted, his hands coming up to block Alex's fists. They rolled in the dirt, a chaotic blur of swinging limbs and raw desperation.

Hank landed a solid uppercut to Alex's jaw, snapping his head sideways. His skull blossomed with pain, making him even angrier. He jabbed a fist into Hank's ribs, knocking the wind out of him. Hank gasped, and Alex seized the advantage.

"Should've left it alone, Hank." Alex drove his fist into Hank's face, over and over again until the older man lay almost motionless beneath him, his breath wet and uneven.

Panting, Alex stumbled to his feet, spotted the knife and picked it up. Turning back to Hank, he hesitated for a moment. The old man was barely conscious, his bloodied face turned up to the cloudy sky.

This hadn't been his intention, but he did pride himself on taking advantage of an opportunity.

"At least the horse got to live," Alex muttered. Then, gripping the knife, he stepped forward to finish the job.

Chapter Thirteen

Erin woke to silence. The wind no longer howled, rain no longer beat upon the cabin's metal roof. Matt spooned her in a cocoon of warmth, his breath on her shoulder a rhythmic pattern of exhalations. She snuggled in closer, and his arms tightened around her in a reassuring embrace.

She'd made the right decision last night.

"Morning." Matt nuzzled her neck, sending a shiver of pleasure through her.

She twisted around in his arms and gazed into his smiling eyes. "Sounds like the storm's over."

"Uh-huh." He kissed her.

"We should probably get going."

"Uh-huh." Another kiss.

As much as Erin would love to spend the day cuddling with Matt in front of a cozy fire, Alex's catastrophe countdown clock ruined the moment. "We've got to search the other areas we marked on the map."

"We will. Right after we—"

Erin turned her cheek with a soft laugh. The other day in the barn, Hank had told her it was past time for her to trust her instincts. And after ten long years, she was finally coming to believe that herself. But part of internalizing that belief was not allowing herself to be controlled by her baser needs. "Search now, play later." She mustered some country-girl fortitude, slipped from his grasp and rose from their makeshift bed.

With an exaggerated sigh, Matt rolled to his feet just in time to catch the clothes Erin tossed to him. "At least they're dry."

"You're dead wrong about that. They're still damp on the inside, but they'll do to get us home." She hopped on one foot, trying to pull on her stiff jeans without straining her sore shoulder. "Man oh man, do I ever need a hot shower. And clean clothes. And food. And lots of coffee."

"And not necessarily in that order." Matt caught Erin as she lost her balance and dragged her back down on the blankets with him.

"Stop that. We can't," she scolded, laughing as he kissed her neck.

"You sure can be stubborn when you want to be." Matt released her and they stood.

She helped him fold the blankets and quilts and set them on a chair. With her jacket and gloves on, Erin stepped into the sunshine and looked up at the cloudless sky. "What a difference a day makes."

Matt locked the cabin door and put the key back in its hiding spot. "Let's hope that's true when we get to the truck." He pulled his phone from his pocket and checked their location. "*If* we can get to the truck."

Erin tapped his phone map to enlarge it. "We can circle around this way to get back to the parking lot."

Trusting her knowledge of the area, Matt followed her in a roundabout detour to the far side of the ravine.

When they reached a washed-out part of the trail, Matt

stated the obvious. "It doesn't look like this route goes through."

Biting her tongue against a sarcastic retort, Erin checked the phone map again. The remnants of a fast-flowing channel of rainwater rushed past them. "We'll need to backtrack and hike farther to the west. Try to find a narrower spot to cross this, then double back on the other side."

They traversed the difficult landscape, climbing past mudslides and negotiating rivulets and streams that didn't exist before the storm.

By the time they arrived at the truck, they were covered in mud. Erin's stomach growled for food and her head throbbed from lack of caffeine. "I think I'm hangry."

Matt kicked at the thick, wet sludge encasing the truck's tires. "Then this won't help."

Erin knew soil in this part of Texas consisted primarily of clay, which wreaked havoc when caked around vehicle tires. Ideally, they'd let it dry and then knock it off, but they didn't have time for that. The other way to clean them was to pressure-wash the thick goop off. Another non-option for them out in the middle of nowhere

"Where's your tire iron?" Erin took off her jacket while Matt rummaged in the back seat and came out with a hammer and the iron. Erin chose the hammer and went to work scraping away the mud.

While she worked, her mind drifted back to the night before. To Matt's soft kisses and gentle touches. To the taste of his mouth, his body. To the intensity ramping up until she flew high and then crashed to the ground, pleasure filling every inch of her body, every corner of her soul.

Erin glanced at Matt, who had worked his way around the truck to her side. With each downward stroke of his tire iron against the mud, her thoughts went to a place they shouldn't be. Not when they needed to get back to the ranch, change clothes and start searching again. So she fought the smile trying to hijack her mouth, averted her eyes and focused on her own tire.

An hour later, the tires were clean enough to rotate within the wheel wells. Matt put the truck into four-wheel drive to navigate the storm-ravaged terrain, and they headed home.

Erin stepped out of the truck, the hairs on the back of her neck standing on end. The ranch was silent, but not in a tranquil way. This stillness pressed on her chest and made it hard to breathe.

"Something's wrong."

But what? She glanced at the bunkhouse, then panned back up the road they'd just driven in on. Nothing to arouse suspicion, and yet her heart jackhammered in her chest. Why? What had her subconscious realized that her waking self was missing?

She heard snorting and turned toward the barn. The door stood open and hooked to the wall. Perfectly normal, and yet from the sounds inside, the horses seemed as uneasy as she was. They pawed at the ground, stomped their hooves.

Without thinking, Erin wandered in that direction, moving with caution.

"What is it?" Matt asked, walking by her side.

"I'm not sure. Maybe nothing." But she didn't think it was nothing, and Matt didn't seem to think so either.

Still a ways out from the open barn door, Erin made out Blaze, Shadow and Redemption standing loose just inside, dried sweat showing on their coats. They whinnied, their ears flicking back and forth.

No, no, no, she screamed inside her head. She sprinted toward the barn, Matt's bodyguard rules forgotten.

"Wait!" he shouted, matching her pace. "What's wrong?"

"Hank wouldn't leave them loose like this. And the only way they'd have sweat residue in this weather is if they've been running."

Matt grabbed hold of her arm and yanked her to a stop, keeping her from rushing headlong inside. "Damn it, Erin. Stop! Let me clear the area first." He pulled his gun from its holster with one hand. With the other, he shoved her behind him. "Maybe Hank's in the back."

They approached Shadow, the nearest horse, who raised her head, shaking it and flaring her nostrils. "No," Erin whispered, a tight knot of tension gripping her chest. "Hank would have groomed them."

Matt pointed out damp areas on the floor. "Looks like the door was open during yesterday's storm. Maybe Hank's sick or hurt himself."

Erin pulled her phone from her pocket and tapped Hank's number. After each ring on her phone, a fainter ring followed from somewhere outside. She pulled open the barn's front door, and she could hear the ring a little better. Her gaze settled on what looked like a pile of rags inside the corral.

"Matt…" Her voice was tight and loaded with fear. She knew firsthand the danger Alex represented, but she'd denied to herself that he would carry through with the worst of his threats.

Please let me be mistaken. Please, please let Hank be all right.

Matt joined her at the door and scanned the scene. "Wait here. Let me check it out."

But Erin ignored him. Her head on a swivel just as Matt's was, she followed him, the frosty morning air stinging her cheeks as together they edged through the open corral gate toward the bundle.

A bundle that was no mere bundle. Her breath caught in her throat. A camel-colored jacket, worn jeans, old boots. A crumpled body in the bloodstained mud. A familiar face, bruised and battered. Eyes milky and lifeless. Erin's knees buckled, and she fell to the ground beside him.

"Hank," she whispered, her voice breaking. Tears blurred her vision as she reached out, her trembling hand stopping just short of his cheek. "Oh, Hank." Her words came out in a low moan as she took in his face, turned to the sky as if he'd been looking to the heavens for help. Help that hadn't come.

"Don't, Erin. Don't touch him." Matt lifted her to her feet. His voice firm but gentle, his hand steady on her shoulder. "It's a crime scene." He pulled his phone from his pocket, his other hand guiding her away from Hank.

"This is Matt Franklin. We need law enforcement at the Montgomery Ranch immediately. Possible homicide," he said into the phone, his tone professional. Then he turned his attention back to Erin.

"He's gone, Matt. Hank's gone."

Matt wrapped his arms around her, pulling her against

his chest. She buried her face in his shoulder, her tears soaking his shirt. "I know," he said, his voice low and soothing. "I'm sorry." He held her as she shook with grief. "I'm so sorry."

Like a collage of pictures projected onto a screen, memories of Hank flashed through Erin's mind.

The first time she sat on a horse, she'd been three. With her mother insisting she was too young, Hank had managed to find a moment when they weren't being watched. He'd lifted her up and held on to her tightly while she experienced what would become her passion. Horses.

Their last conversation, just a few days earlier in the barn. Hank had urged her to trust her instincts. He'd always had more faith in her than she had in herself. And he had also been right about Matt. About the attraction between her and her bodyguard.

When Hank had observed things happening on the ranch, he hadn't just seen them at surface level. His perception had run deeper, allowing him to counsel Erin with down-to-earth cowboy wisdom. Hank had been her anchor. And now, without him, she was adrift.

The weight of her loss crushed Erin as she tried to process the impossible reality. Hank, her friend, the steady presence in her life since childhood, was gone. One more casualty of her past. She could barely breathe around the pain.

With his arm still around her, Matt said, "We should go wait on the porch for the police."

Erin let him guide her away, each step farther from Hank more difficult than the last.

"You know as well as I do, Alex did this," she said, not surprised by the rage bubbling deep inside her. But the amount of anger she harbored toward Matt *did* catch her off guard. If they'd left the ravine when she wanted to, Alex's confrontation might have been with a bodyguard trained for such situations instead of an innocent old man. She kept her feelings to herself, however. Matt was still her protector, and her only ally in finding the jewelry and ending Alex's reign of terror.

After settling her on the porch swing, Matt crouched in front of her, his eyes filled with concern. "And we'll make sure he winds up back in prison." Matt took her hand. "Just remember, I'm here with you. You don't have to handle any of this alone."

Erin clung to those words, but it was like grasping a small raft engulfed by the raging floodwaters of her grief. Hank had been more than a ranch hand. More than a friend and confidant. He had been family.

And now, because of her, he had died a violent, painful death. How could she ever forgive herself for that?

MATT WALKED OVER to the corral as flashing lights illuminated the ranch. The grounds had become a grim hive of activity, with police officers from Winston taking photographs of the scene and marking evidence with yellow placards.

What was it Erin had said just hours earlier—what a difference a day makes?

Ain't that the truth. From a storm to clear skies to murder in less than twenty-four hours. He went over those hours in his mind, guilt clawing its way through him. They had no idea yet what time Hank had been killed. And Matt had no control over the previous day's weather. But he should have heeded Erin's warning about a potential gully washer instead of insisting they'd be fine. It had been his fault she almost drowned during the storm. His fault they hadn't made it back to the ranch last night, possibly in time to save Hank.

And what if he and Erin had been making love at the same time a knife was draining the life force from the man? Matt's self-reproach deepened with the realization he was enjoying last night while Hank may have been lying out here, gasping his last few breaths.

His job was to protect *Erin*. But by not protecting all of those she loved, he'd exposed her to the results of Alex Townsend's savagery. Something she'd have to live with for the rest of her life. Matt had secured protection for the O'Roarkes. He should have pushed harder to keep Hank safe somehow.

But from here on, Erin and Matt would be joined at the hip. If Alex intended to hurt Erin, Matt would see him coming a mile away.

He looked toward the bunkhouse, where Erin sat on the porch steps, knees pulled to her chest, arms wrapped around her legs. Her eyes, puffy from crying, focused on the spot where Hank's lifeless body still lay. Matt's chest tightened at the sight of her, although he'd learned she was tougher than she looked. It would be difficult, but she'd survive this. He hoped their relationship would survive it, too.

"Mr. Franklin?" A young Winston officer approached him, appearing a bit overwhelmed. From what Matt had heard, murders weren't exactly commonplace out here. "Detective Martinez would like to ask you a few questions. If you'll come with me?"

Matt nodded, and after one last glance at Erin, followed the baby-faced officer to where Detective Martinez stood, holding a pen and a small notepad. The woman, who looked to be in her late thirties, was tall and imposing. Experience radiated from eyes darting here and there, taking in everything, trying to make sense of the senseless. She gave Matt a sharp nod as he approached.

"Mr. Franklin, I understand you're Ms. Montgomery's bodyguard. You work for Nate Reed over at Resolute Security?" Martinez asked, her voice calm but firm.

"Yes, ma'am."

"Can you walk me through what happened here?"

Scrubbing a hand across his face, Matt gave Martinez a concise replay of the morning's events.

Martinez scribbled in her notepad. "So, neither of you saw or heard anything unusual before coming outside?"

"No. We didn't come from the house. We got caught in yesterday's storm, hunkered down for the night and didn't make it back until this morning. When we arrived, Erin, um, my client, felt that something seemed…" He paused, searching for the right word. "Off."

Martinez gave him a nonjudgmental, but curious, look. "Where did you say you spent the night?"

He hadn't said, but best not to quibble with this all-business detective. "In a vacant hunter's cabin. We found the key hidden on the porch and let ourselves in. We left the place in the same condition we found it." Better to possibly get in trouble for illegal entry than become a murder suspect.

"I'll need you and Ms. Montgomery to come to the station later to make complete statements, including details about your entire day yesterday." She looked up from her pad. "I understand you both believe Alex Townsend should be considered a suspect in the death of Hank Caldwell."

"Yes, we do."

Martinez gave a noncommittal nod. "So, you were with Ms. Montgomery all night since you were hired to protect her from Alex Townsend's harassment. Correct?"

Matt's jaw tightened. He resented the implication in the detective's *all night* word choice, but he knew this line of questioning was necessary. Warranted. "Twenty-four/seven protection. Yes, ma'am."

She scribbled more notes, then gave him a hard look. "So, what can you tell me about Alex that I won't find in the police reports?"

"You've probably heard about the robbery back—"

She cut him off. "I know all about that."

Appreciating her brevity, Matt said, "Right. Well, since getting out of prison, Townsend has been making threats all week. Your department took a report on him for intimidating Liam O'Roarke and his wife. Here, I can provide you with a case number." He took out his phone, made a few swipes, then showed her a screen. "Resolute Security has provided protection for the O'Roarkes, but I'll be talking to my boss about tightening it."

Martinez jotted down the number. "Anything else?"

"Yes. He made another threat using one of my client's riding students." Matt filled in the detective on the incident with Tommy's marble and Alex pretending to be Hank for access to the bunkhouse. "I think you should send someone over to the Barrows household, provide protection for Tommy and his mother, Jill."

"Why didn't you file a report about that?" Martinez narrowed her eyes at him.

"I did. The officer I spoke with said he'd take my statement, but he needed proof it was Townsend. Said I was just speculating on the identity of the perp."

Martinez blew out a sharp breath. "We'll look into it. Do you have security footage on the property?"

"Yes. I'll show you." Matt slogged through the mud in the corral as he led the detective to the gate. He pointed up. "We installed cameras on two of these light posts, one facing the barn, the other aimed at the bunkhouse. And we have several on top of the barn and the bunkhouse. We also added a couple to catch the back of the two buildings." He indicated the trees marking the end of the road from the front gate.

Police officers crisscrossed the area, consulting with each other. Twice, Matt and Martinez were stopped so officers could clarify something with the detective. Glancing at Hank's body, Matt noticed a policewoman photographing and measuring footprints in the mud. *Erin and I will have to show them our shoes in order to exclude us from any suspicious prints.*

A justice of the peace stood by the corral gate, drumming his fingers on the top rail while waiting for the police to finish their footprint evidence collection before declaring Hank dead. Matt had learned that Boone County didn't have a coroner. The Harris County crime lab in Houston would perform the autopsy and handle the forensic investigation.

As Matt and Martinez finally approached the bunkhouse, he met Erin's eyes. She seemed lost amid all the chaos, and her gaze held the remnants of the morning's horror. But a glint of hope also shone in them. That, along with the determined set of her mouth, told him she still had a lot of fight left in her. And he intended to fight right alongside her.

After climbing the porch steps, Matt rested his hand on Erin's shoulder for a moment. As he gave a gentle squeeze, she covered his hand with hers. His resolve to keep her safe from that maniac Townsend tripled in strength.

Matt and Martinez sat on the bunkhouse couch while he pulled up the footage on his computer. Erin, despite her fragile state, insisted on joining them.

"You don't have to watch this." Matt worried what witnessing any portion of the violent death of her friend would do to her state of mind. Once seen, something that soul-stealing could never be unseen.

"I *need* to," she insisted, her voice raw with emotion.

Camera one, located on one of the tall light posts near the corral, showed Hank leading two horses out of the barn, then slapping their rumps to send them running. Then he drew his gun and ran toward the corral. There was nothing more until Redemption tore through the frame in the same direction the other horses had gone.

Although disappointed the footage provided no clues to the murder itself, Matt was glad Erin hadn't seen anything too traumatic.

Erin's breath hitched as the video looped again to Hank running. "That's the last time I…" Her voice broke as she stared at the screen.

To hell with Martinez and whatever she might think the relationship was between Matt and his client. He wrapped an arm around Erin's shoulders, his heart hurting for her. This was wrong on so many levels. He was breaking his word to Nate. He was setting himself up for another monumental fall. But in this moment, he didn't care.

Martinez leaned back, an unreadable expression on her face. "Do you have footage from any other angles?"

Hoping Townsend had been caught on camera on his way to the murder scene, Matt ran the recordings from every camera he'd had installed. But no luck. It seemed the killer knew how to avoid them all. "We focused on the buildings and areas between them rather than the corral."

Martinez stood. "Convenient for our perp that the storm washed away physical evidence," she muttered, more to herself than anyone else. "I'll need a copy of all this footage, as well as from the front gate camera, for us to review more thoroughly. But I'll be frank, Ms. Montgomery. Without more evidence or witnesses, we have nothing to charge Alex Townsend with."

Erin's large brown eyes glistened through her tears. She looked up at Martinez, pleading with the detective to believe her. "I'm telling you, it was Alex."

Martinez nodded. "So I've noted. I run my investigations by the book, Ms. Montgomery, but I can assure you we will be looking into him as a person of interest."

Erin's shoulders sagged beneath Matt's arm.

They returned to the porch, where Matt stayed close to Erin, comforting her, while the police continued their work. They both knew who had done this. Now it was a matter of proving it.

Chapter Fourteen

Thursday dawned with a cloudless sky, too bright and clear for a funeral. To Erin, it seemed the weather should be as bleak and gloomy as she felt. The past three days had crept by in a blur for her.

As requested, she and Matt had visited the Winston police station to give their statements. Planning Hank's funeral had taken much longer than she'd expected. As had exercising Blaze and Shadow and working with Redemption without Hank's assistance. Matt had helped with her two horses while she fought back tears each time she'd taken out the dressage horse.

Taking into account the time difference, Erin had called her parents to let them know about Hank. Although upset, they couldn't come home for the funeral because of her dad's business obligations. But their worry for her had been evident. Her mother had insisted on talking to Matt, and apparently made it clear that if anything happened to their daughter, Matt would regret ever setting foot in Texas.

Erin and Matt had also managed a few more searches but found nothing, and a layer of dread rested just beneath her grief. Time was running out, and the question of whom Alex's next victim might be tormented her.

Erin entered the Cowboy Church of Boone County, Matt tight at her side, and made her way to the front row of folding chairs in the rustic barn that served as a place of worship. All of the hands who worked at the Montgomery Ranch were there, filling the first few rows. The rest of the room held everyone who'd known Hank and wanted to pay their respects. Not a suit in sight, just jeans, pearl button shirts and cowboy boots. Hank would be honored.

"Did you see Detective Martinez when we came in?" Matt whispered.

"Yes. She told me they'd keep a plainclothes officer with Jill and Tommy during the funeral and have more at the graveside service, too." Erin twisted a tissue between her fingers. "I just hope Alex shows up and they catch him without anyone else getting hurt."

"I'm more concerned that he'll take advantage of no one being at the ranch. Nate texted me earlier. He, Luke and Gabe have set up there and will keep watch until we all return," Matt said.

"Who are Luke and Gabe?" Erin asked, confused.

"Two of my fellow bodyguards at Resolute Security. There are four of us now, but Nate wants to hire more down the road." Matt leaned sideways and asked in a low voice, "How are Maeve and Liam doing at Hidden Oaks?"

"They're safe, but… Let's just say it's been an adjustment for them."

The O'Roarkes had moved into a double room at the facility, with both the hired guard Nate had arranged for and Resolute Security's Charlie with them round the clock. Erin appreciated the immediate increase in security after Hank's death, but after so many years of living apart, Liam complained to her that he felt stifled by Maeve's close attention. No more Irish whiskey for him.

A small grin tugged at Erin's mouth as she thought about the ruckus Liam had caused when his disapproving wife discovered his secret stashes. She'd removed all his contraband from the premises, despite Liam's loud and heated protests of their medicinal properties.

Somber music from a small country band pulled Erin away from her memory, and she braced herself for the funeral.

First, the hymns. "The Old Rugged Cross," "How Great Thou Art" and "Amazing Grace." Familiar songs that brought tears of sadness for the finality of death. But also brought comfort, at least for Erin. Bible readings proclaimed the promised hope of the afterlife, and friends stood and recounted stories that spoke of Hank's impeccable character and his abiding loyalty. The preacher then signaled Erin. She tensed, and Matt squeezed her hand before she rose and walked to the podium.

She took a deep breath and unfolded a paper with her notes. But then she realized her love for Hank didn't require her to read from notes after all. The words flowed directly from her heart. "Hank was like a grandfather to me in every way but blood," she began, her voice only quavering a little. "He may have been a paid ranch hand, but it wasn't in his job description to teach me to ride, to shoot. All the physical skills needed to run a successful ranch. Nor was it in his job description to bandage my scraped knees, wrap my sprained wrists and ankles and once, when I was twelve, promise me that I wasn't going to die when a horse stepped on my foot." Erin gave a small shrug. "What can I say? As a child, I had a tendency to be accident prone."

Chuckles and knowing nods came from Hank's friends and neighbors. Erin smiled out at them, tears forming in her eyes. The back of her throat was so tight it ached, and she took the moment to compose herself. Anyone who knew Hank had, at one point or another, been on the receiving end of his gruff but loving ministrations and generous nature.

She gripped the sides of the podium, steadied herself and continued. "But what he taught me that I value so much more than how to care for animals, how to operate farm machinery or the physical labor needed to build muscles on my skinny frame—" she mimicked Hank's voice on that last one, which earned another round of small chuckles "—were life's intangibles. Attributes like loyalty, persistence and fortitude. But most of all, love. John 15:13 says there is no greater love than to lay down one's life for one's friends. And that's just what Hank did. He saved three horses, protected the ranch and…and he gave his life to protect me."

Erin wasn't sure what people knew about the circumstances of Hank's death. They knew he had been murdered. By now everyone knew that. But what else did they know? That Alex was the prime suspect? And even if they did, did they remember him as one of the people arrested with Erin on that night ten years ago?

In Erin's mind, what they knew or didn't know wasn't important. What mattered was that Hank fought off Alex to protect her, and she would be forever grateful to him.

And for the rest of her life, she would miss his steadfast presence. But thanks to his wise guidance, she was not blaming herself for his death. Not anymore. Though no proof existed that Alex was the culprit, in her heart of hearts, she believed he was. And if it was the last thing she did, she would see to it that Alex paid the price.

She looked skyward. "Thank you," she said to Hank in a choked whisper. "For everything. I'm going to miss you so, so much."

Tears streamed down her cheeks, and she could barely speak. "I love you," was all she managed. After that, she was incapable of saying more and returned to her seat.

Thankfully, her tears during the brief service ended with an uplifting message from the preacher. Pallbearers removed the coffin, and the crowd filed out of the building. Erin spotted Jill, Tommy and their policewoman escort, another harsh reminder of why they were all here today.

"I want to say a few words to Jill," Erin said.

Matt nodded, and they approached the trio.

Jill gave Erin a hug. "I'm so sorry. Tommy always looked forward to seeing Hank during his riding lessons."

Tommy tipped his head back to look up at Matt. "I lost my big marble, but want to see what I found the other day?"

"I sure do." Matt waited while Tommy dug in his pocket. "Sorry about your marble."

"It's okay. This is way better." The young boy held his hand up, something sparkling between his thumb and forefinger.

Erin, listening to Jill's condolences while at the same time keeping tabs on Tommy's conversation with Matt, turned her attention to the ring. "Can I see that?"

With only a small hesitation, he handed it to her, and Erin's stomach clenched.

"Why, this is beautiful," she said, not wanting the boy to become reluctant to share. "Like a pirate's treasure. Where on earth did you find this?" Erin rotated the diamond cocktail ring, sunlight flashing from its faceted surfaces.

Tommy glanced up at his mom before looking at his feet.

"Tommy?" Jill frowned at her son, waiting until he raised his eyes to hers. "It's okay. I promise you're not in any trouble. Tell her the truth, Tommy."

The boy hesitated, then hemmed and hawed.

Jill looked at Erin, her brow furrowed, then Matt squatted down to Tommy's level as if he sensed something wasn't going right. "Hey, man, I think this ring might be very, very important. Maybe even a clue to a hidden treasure." Matt gave him a conspiratorial smile. "Can you tell me where you got it?"

"I found it outside that old abandoned mine," Tommy said in an eager voice. "You know, the one with a tree on each side?"

"You mean the one with a live tree on one side and a dead one on the other?" Erin asked.

"Yeah, yeah. That's the one. It was the day before the storm."

Erin crouched down next to Matt. "Are you sure about that?"

"Uh-huh, Miss Erin. I remember 'cause my mom doesn't let me play outside after it rains on account of I always get so muddy."

"I see." Erin smiled at the thought of Tommy covered in mud.

"Yeah, so like I was over there, and I was digging up rocks like Indiana Jones 'cause I'm gonna be an archaeologist just like him, and I was near the entrance and saw this shiny thing."

"An archaeologist? That's cool," Matt said. "You're sure it was outside the mine? Not inside?"

Tommy nodded. "I'm not allowed to go inside the mine 'cause it's all boarded up. Mom said it might collapse on me and then she'd never find me."

"She's absolutely right about that. I'm glad you listened to her. I bet even Indiana Jones wouldn't go inside that mine." Erin held up the ring. "Would it be okay if I borrow this for a little while?"

"Um… Yeah, I guess so." Tommy's reply was soft. "But you'll give it back to me, right? 'Cause I found it, and you know, finders keepers."

"I'll be honest, if it's what I think it is, I might have to give it to the police," Erin said. "But if that happens, you'll be a hero, and heroes get rewards."

"They do? So, maybe I could get another riding lesson?" His gaze slid to his mother before whispering, "Mom says we can't afford any more for a while."

Jill's cheeks flushed, but before she could refute Tommy's claim, Erin spoke up.

"Tommy, if I can't give this back to you, I'll give you free riding lessons for as long as you want to take them."

The boy's face lit up with delight. "You want me to see if I can find more stuff out there?"

"No. It would be safer for you to stay away from the

mine for now." Erin held his shoulders and looked him straight in the eye. "Promise?"

Tommy scrunched up his face and looked away.

Erin pressed him. "You want free riding lessons, don't you?"

"I sure do."

"Good. Then promise me. You won't go back to the mine."

"Okay, I promise." His serious expression segued into an enormous smile. "Anything for more lessons."

Erin stood, and Matt followed suit, his knees popping in protest.

As Jill gave her friend another hug, she whispered, "This is so embarrassing, but I do appreciate the offer."

"Don't be silly," Erin said. "I've missed Tommy as much as he's missed riding."

"Thank you." The two women separated. "Again, I'm so very sorry about Hank." Jill took Tommy's hand and led him toward the parking lot, the vigilant police officer walking alongside.

"Is that a part of what I think it is?" Matt asked.

"I sure hope so." Erin pocketed the ring, its weight feeling heavier than its few ounces of metal and gemstone. "We need to hurry and get to the cemetery for the graveside service."

Erin noticed Matt's jaw tighten subtly. Lately, she'd found him easier to read.

"Something wrong?"

"I'm just not a big fan of funerals. Especially the part by the grave." Matt gave her a tight smile. "Don't worry. It's not a big deal."

She slipped her hand into his. "So, tell me. Who did you lose?"

For a moment, it seemed he didn't intend to answer. "My mom," he finally said, the two muted words conveying a loss that still hurt him.

"I'm sorry." Erin realized she knew very little about the man she'd been sleeping with the past few nights.

"It was a long time ago." He got her into his truck and then joined the line of vehicles proceeding to the cemetery.

"What about your father? Is he still alive?"

"Unfortunately, yes." The bitterness of his words shocked Erin.

"I take it you're not close?"

An ugly laugh broke loose from Matt's throat. "You could say that. We haven't seen or spoken to each other in twenty years."

"I'm sorry to hear that."

"Don't be. He's in prison." He glanced at her before turning his attention back to the vehicle in front of them. "For killing my mom."

Whatever Erin might have imagined as the reason for the rift between Matt and his father, never in a million years would she have guessed that. To lose your mother at the hands of your father. She couldn't begin to understand what that had done to the boy he'd been.

"Oh, Matt. I'm so sorry." Her words seemed so grossly inadequate, but what could one say when told something like that? What she did know was that her heart, already shattered from losing Hank, broke a little more.

"Like I said, it was a long time ago."

"How old were you?" Her voice came out in a whisper.

"Nine. The police arrested him for beating her up, but she took him back anyway. That's when he killed her." Matt's voice took on an even darker tone. "When she gave him a second chance."

MATT'S ANXIETY METER flashed red after the long, emotional day, and he was on high alert. Alex had crossed a line with Hank's murder. And now that he had, chances were high that if the killer didn't get what he wanted, he would kill again.

Not Erin, necessarily. Alex still needed her to find the jewels, but almost anyone else who attended the funeral services was at risk. And that's what worried him, because Erin also knew that. Matt's worst fear was that she would put herself in harm's way to protect those she cared about. Just like Hank had done.

On the way home, Matt called Nate for a ranch update.

"Everything's quiet here. Some of the guys who work here are returning to the big bunkhouse, so I've pulled Luke. The ranch hands all know who to watch for." Nate spoke to someone near him, then came back on the phone. "No activity near the big house or the barn and bunkhouse where you and Erin are staying. Winston police are posting one officer across the road from your bunkhouse for the night, so we're headed back to Resolute."

"Thanks, boss. Maybe we can finally unwind a little." Matt favored Erin with a weak smile. Despite her tears and anguish since Hank's murder, today she'd remained brave, determined to make the day only about the deceased. Oh, she had shed tears, and plenty of them. But she'd been able to give a fine eulogy for her friend. It seemed to be catching up with her, but his heart lightened when she gave him a faint smile in return.

"Here's hoping you do. Stay vigilant."

"Always. I'll keep you posted on any developments." Matt ended the call just as they approached the main gate.

Erin sighed. "All I want to do tonight is curl up on the couch in my warmest pajamas, have a beer and not cry."

Matt glanced at her again, her face the picture of exhaustion as she ran her fingers through her hair. "You grab the pajamas, I'll grab the beers."

"That sounds perfect." She paused. "Thank you, Matt."

"For what?"

"For being there with me today."

"It's my job."

"That's not what I mean." Erin gave him a pointed look.

"I know." He gave her hand a gentle squeeze. "And you're welcome."

It was testament to her exhaustion that Erin didn't even try to get out of the truck before Matt opened her door. Or maybe Hank's death had impressed upon her the need to adhere to safety protocols. Whatever the reason, he appreciated her cooperation. Made his job that much easier and lowered his anxiety by a notch.

With an arm around her, he ushered her into the bunkhouse and made her wait by the locked door while he cleared every room.

"No unwanted visitors," he said.

After toeing off her boots, she trudged to her bedroom like a zombie. By the time Matt sat on the couch with two open bottles of beer, Erin had already collapsed on it. He pulled her against him, wrapping his arm around her.

"I sure am going to miss him." Erin tapped her bottle against Matt's. "To Hank."

"To Hank," Matt echoed.

They sipped in silence, letting the toast fill the space between them.

After a beat, Matt broke the quiet. "Will you bring someone from the main stables over here to work with your horses?"

Erin shook her head. "I can't ask anyone else to risk their lives. For now, I can take care of them myself." She turned her head and smiled at Matt. "Especially if you keep helping me."

"I'll remind you that shoveling horse manure is absolutely *not* in my job description."

"City boy."

"Country hick."

"A country hick who will have you shoveling manure in no time."

"Says you."

"Says me." Erin kissed him on the cheek.

Their enjoyable banter lapsed into silence, and Matt's thoughts returned to their current situation. "You told me how much Hank and Alex disliked each other. Could Hank's death have been a personal vendetta and not part of Alex's quest for the missing loot?"

Erin blew out a hard breath. "Maybe, but I don't think so, and I'm not endangering another hand on the ranch by recruiting one of them."

They again settled into a comfortable silence, Matt replaying the day's events in his head. Erin leaned against his shoulder, her eyes half-closed. Matt liked her nearness. Liked it too much for his own good.

Throughout the day, they had held hands in public several times, and Matt doubted that anyone who saw them confused Matt's job as Erin's bodyguard with the fact that he'd developed genuine feelings for her. Nate was going to come unglued.

Matt knew that by allowing his relationship with Erin to grow, he could be putting his partnership in Resolute Security in jeopardy. And yet, he felt powerless to stop. No, not powerless, he corrected. Unwilling. "So, you really think the ring Tommy had is part of the stolen jewelry?"

"I can't believe I forgot about it." Erin jumped up, retrieved the ring and dropped back down on the couch. "Here." She handed him the piece. "Since he found it near the mine, and the mine is near the ravine we searched, I'll bet you anything that's where the loot's hidden. I say we search the mine first thing tomorrow morning."

Matt's longed-for tranquility slammed into a brick wall. "Erin, listen to me. That mine is boarded up for a reason. It's too dangerous, and we're not going inside."

And there was his mistake. Telling her instead of asking this complicated, adorable, stubborn, caring woman not to do this.

She stiffened, moved off his shoulder and gave him a look of such intensity that he knew what she planned to say before she opened her mouth. Just as he knew he absolutely did not want to hear it.

"I'm going. If there's even a sliver of a chance the loot's there, it'll be worth the risk." Determination laced Erin's voice, and Matt knew he was sunk. "Alex has already hurt too many innocent people, and I refuse to let Hank's sacrifice be for nothing."

"Erin, try to be reasonable—" *Another mistake.*

"What?" She got to her feet, each fist stubbornly planted on her hips.

"Calm down. All I meant—" *And yet another mistake.*

"Calm down? Hank is dead, we finally have our first real clue, and you want me to ignore it?"

"Yes, I do. We can report it to the police and wait for them to send in a professional search and rescue team."

"Alex isn't waiting, and neither am I."

There was a finality in her declaration. Still, Matt had to try to make her see reason. "The police will catch Alex, and he'll be back in prison in no time."

She narrowed her eyes. "The evidence against him is circumstantial. You said so yourself. What happens if the police question him and have to let him go? He'll be angrier and even more vengeful. So what would we gain except potentially putting more people in harm's way?"

Reasoning with Erin wasn't working. Time to put his foot down. Matt rose from the couch and crossed the room to the small kitchen. "We're not searching the mine. My job is to protect *you*. And whether that's from Alex Townsend or your own misguided ideas, I intend to do just that." Opening the fridge, he asked, "You want another beer?"

"No, thank you. I need a clear head to finish this conversation."

He shrugged. "Suit yourself." He hoped taking his time would dampen her hostility, so he popped the cap off, then returned to the couch at a leisurely pace.

Erin glared at him. "And exactly what did you mean by 'protecting me from my own misguided ideas'?"

Matt closed his eyes. *Jeez.* How was he supposed to

continue this conversation without upsetting her even more? "Erin, I swear. I understand your concern, but you need to understand mine. This guy isn't just hurting people now. He's killing them." Matt patted the couch cushion, wanting her to sit back down next to him. To hear what he was saying, to heed his warnings. She didn't.

"That's my point. We have to do whatever we can to make sure he doesn't kill anyone else."

"The authorities are looking for Alex as a person of interest in Hank's death. In the meantime, we have eyes on everyone who you've deemed a potential target. If Alex shows up, we'll nab him."

"Great. So, that's your plan? We wait?"

"Yes, and while we wait, I believe we should limit our movements to the bunkhouse, barn and corral."

"So, you're turning me into a prisoner on the ranch, even more so than my mother did."

"That's not fair."

"No more unfair than what you're suggesting."

He wasn't suggesting anything but decided not to press the point. "Erin—"

"So, what happens if Alex doesn't show up? What then? Why not search the mine as a backup plan?"

Damn it, he didn't want to scare her, but at this point he didn't think he had a choice. Not if he was going to keep her in one piece. "With Alex escalating his threats and time running out, I'm concerned he'll come after you."

"If you come to the mine with me, there's no reason why you can't protect me there the same as you can protect me here."

"Think, Erin. There are cameras here. Alarms. Help within minutes. Out there, we're isolated. And once we set foot in that mine, we're at the mercy of crumbling shafts and falling debris." Matt crossed his arms over his chest. "I believe the rational thing to do is just stay here and let the police catch Alex."

But it seemed only one word penetrated Erin's brain.

"So now I'm misguided *and* irrational? Have I got that right?"

"No, that's not what I... I guess I wasn't clear about what I meant."

Erin stalked to her bedroom. "Well, let's see if *this* is clear enough for *you*." She went in and slammed the door behind her, the lock clicking loudly into place.

I guess it's back to the junk room for me.

EVEN WITH BONE-CRUSHING EXHAUSTION, Erin couldn't fall asleep. She stared at the ceiling, indignant, hurt and angry. Matt had been willing to search the long shots, like the ranch and the gully. But now, with their best clue so far for the most likely hiding spot of the jewelry, he shut the whole thing down. He expected her to listen, to be rational, to understand the safety concerns. But he didn't listen to her. Just like he hadn't listened to her about the storm in the ravine, and she'd been 100 percent right about it. He didn't respect her decisions. He didn't understand her intensified desire to find the jewelry.

Jill and Tommy had police protection. Liam and Maeve had top-of-the-line security. Hank was dead. The only person close to Erin that Alex could go after now was Matt himself. The man Erin was, without a doubt, falling for. Alex would only have to take one look at her face when Matt was around, and he'd know she was in love.

And Erin was about to blow that.

Matt had already caught her trying to sneak away once. When he caught her again, and she had no doubt he would eventually, she'd lose the trust of Mr. I-Don't-Believe-In-Second-Chances. No way would he forgive her. And after tonight, he'd be watching her like a hawk. She'd wracked her brain trying to figure another way out of this mess, but after hours in the dark, only two options remained. Either she broke his trust and he lived or she kept his trust only to lose him to Alex's madness.

Not really a choice at all.

Chapter Fifteen

After a few hours of sleep, Erin performed a replay of her first covert escape. Confirming that Matt had gone back to his air bed, she disarmed the security system, saddled Shadow by headlamp and took off for the mine. She would have preferred driving, but the truck engine would awaken Matt.

The full moon lit the way as she guided Shadow alongside roads, watching for vehicles or any sort of lights. Once at the mine, she draped the horse's reins around a tree branch and approached the entrance. Bright yellow danger tape crisscrossed plywood boards bolted into the rock that barred access.

One attempt at pulling off the plywood with her gloved hands, and Erin returned to Shadow to retrieve her folding spade and a crowbar. With the crowbar's help, she pried a piece of board away until it cracked in two. Exposed to the elements for years, the wood continued to crack and splinter, and soon she had an opening large enough to walk through.

Not sure what she'd need inside, Erin tossed the spade, crowbar and an empty saddlebag through the opening, patted her zippered pocket for the flashlight and turned on her headlamp. She squeezed past the broken pieces of plywood and entered the mine, the air turning cool and damp. Her light's beam danced across enormous spiderwebs and rough walls streaked with memories of mineral deposits.

The shaft's wooden support beams creaked above her, and each step she took stirred dust that hung suspended in the air. She pulled her bandanna up to cover her mouth and nose as she ventured deeper inside.

Erin followed the main shaft until it split into smaller tunnels. Ducking beneath a low beam, she chose the passage farthest to the left. The walls closed in around her, and when her headlamp flickered, she tapped it until the light steadied.

She came to a cave-in that blocked part of the tunnel. Her pulse sped up as she squeezed past the collapse, every sound exaggerated: loose debris as it slid to the ground, the creaking wood supporting the shaft, even her own breathing. Each step was a gamble, but one she intended to win.

The tunnel continued to narrow, and Erin walked hunched over for as long as she could before dropping to her knees and crawling, pushing her bag and tools ahead of her. After a few minutes, she stopped to catch her breath, glad she didn't suffer from claustrophobia, but the enormity of this escapade suddenly hit her. The mine had been boarded up because it was dangerous. She'd already passed one cave-in. No one knew where she was.

Well, Matt would figure it out fast enough, but he'd be so mad at her, he might just leave her here.

For a moment, Erin considered giving up and returning to the entrance, but she couldn't even if she wanted to. Only a contortionist could turn around in the small space. She pulled her bandanna back up over her mouth and crawled forward, sharp rocks bruising her knees.

Her breath hitched when the tunnel appeared to end ahead of her. The headlamp flickered again, and she struggled to get her flashlight out of her pocket. The brighter beam revealed not a solid wall or another cave-in, but an opening ahead. Relief washed over her, and she pushed through the hole and emerged in an enormous cavern, its floor littered with rocks and loose debris.

Shining her flashlight around, she noticed a pile of rocks on the far side of the room. It seemed unnatural. Out of place. Man-made. She ran to it and pulled away rocks, tossing them to the side. Her excitement grew as she uncovered a black plastic bag hidden under the rubble.

Erin pulled off her gloves and grabbed hold of the bag, only for it to disintegrate in her fingers. But within the shreds of plastic, jewelry glittered in her flashlight's beam.

She retrieved her saddlebag from where she'd dropped it and loaded the jewelry into it until the weight of the bag equaled the weight of her regrets. As she worked, a distant rumble vibrated, and dust rained down on her.

In a panic, she scrambled toward the tunnel. Erin retraced her route in reverse, again pushing the tools and bag ahead of her. She had almost reached the area of the cave-in she'd passed on her way in when more rumbles and vibrations surrounded her. She ran to the space she'd squeezed through earlier. The ground shook. Dirt fell in her eyes. Mid-step through the tight passage, it collapsed.

Everything went dark except the excruciating pain in her shoulder. That blazed with the brightness of a million suns. Dust filled her mouth, her nose, her lungs. Coughing, choking, her eyes watering, Erin suddenly knew what it was like to be buried alive. And standing up, at that.

If her situation weren't so terrifying, the irony might make her laugh. After finally finding the jewelry, she was now buried with it.

But she refused to surrender to the circumstances. She had raised her good arm to chest level in a pushing position when the cave-in happened. An empty space right below it allowed a tiny amount of movement. She pawed at the debris with that hand. Dust thickened the small amount of available air. Each inhale made her cough out more oxygen than she took in. Sweat ran down her face, turning the dirt on it into mud. A small hole appeared, and she put her lips to it, trying to pull in a breath of air.

But it wasn't enough. She couldn't breathe.

Even the fresh pain in her dislocated shoulder faded away as her entire world turned black.

"ERIN!" MATT'S SHOUT echoed through the mine.

When there was no answer, part of his anger turned to worry. Erin had snuck out on him again. Put herself in danger because of Alex as well as the hazardous mine. Put Matt's reputation as a security specialist at risk. He was still mostly furious with her, but concern had definitely joined the party.

Matt continued deeper into the mine. "Erin!" Either she didn't want to answer him or she couldn't. If it was the first, she'd be sorry. If the latter… He wouldn't allow himself to consider that. Not yet, anyway. Instead, he kept going, calling her name, until he came to multiple tunnels branching off in different directions. "Erin!"

Still no response.

Starting with the first smaller tunnel to his right, he went to the mouth of each one. Examined the floor for recent footprints, any clue that might point the way. Matt yelled her name at the top of his lungs into every one of them. When he reached the last one, he noticed disturbances in the dirt at its entrance. After he took several steps into it, his flashlight revealed boot prints that could be Erin's.

He called her name again. This time, he felt vibrations through his feet. He heard a sound he couldn't identify. A cloud of dust rolled toward him from the belly of the mine. Moving as quickly as he could, Matt kept going until his light bounced against a solid wall of dirt and rocks.

Damn it.

He'd chosen the wrong path. But before turning around, he approached the wall to confirm its solidness. There was a small hole, about chin level. Trying not to think about snakes or any other Texas critters that might be inside that hole, Matt pushed his finger through it.

And felt something soft.

Something that felt like…lips?

"Erin?" As he pulled his finger out, Matt hooked it on the edge of the hole and pulled more dirt away. After a few more times of doing that, he shone his flashlight into the hole. Still couldn't see. He shoved two fingers in and pulled. Then four. Then his whole hand. He tried the flashlight again. This time, it revealed part of a face. A nose streaked with dust. A mouth that he would recognize anywhere, even covered with granules of dirt and sand.

But Erin wasn't responding.

How long had she been without air? Matt dug his hand through the hole and pulled. Instead of the hole getting bigger, dirt and debris from around it slid down, hiding her face again. Matt kept clawing at the cave-in, his arms moving like a windmill. One after the other. Never slowing. Never stopping.

As the mess piled up around his legs, Erin began to sag. Matt wrapped an arm around her waist and pulled her to him. Limp as a wilted flower, she slumped against him, her head lolling to the side. She wasn't breathing.

Matt felt for a pulse. Weak, but it was there.

He backed away from the cave-in and laid her on a relatively clean part of the tunnel floor and began CPR. Each time anxiety threatened to seize control, Matt pushed it away.

I don't have time to panic.

Alternating between chest compressions and breaths, Matt fought to save her life. When not holding her nose and breathing into her mouth, he muttered to the count of the compressions.

"You-bet-ter-wake-up-you're-in-so-much-trou-ble-I'm-fur-i-ous-with-you-you-broke-rule-num-ber-one-don't-leave-me-now-I-love-you."

During the second round of compressions, Erin sputtered, coughed out dusty spit, then inhaled a breath. Matt sat back on his haunches, fighting back tears of relief.

Erin looked up at him, dragging a filthy hand across her dirty mouth. "I found the jewelry."

Matt stared at her in silence for a moment and then got to his feet. "What the hell were you thinking?" His angry tone wiped her excited smile right off her face. "I told you to stay away from here!"

"I had to find it." Erin coughed out more dust while she sat up, then stood, unsteady and flinching when she moved her shoulder. "Alex can't keep hurting everyone I care about." Her voice sounded like gravel in a tin cup.

"You injured your shoulder again, didn't you?"

"No." She walked over to the cave-in and dug through the debris with one hand.

Matt followed her. "Yes, you did." He took hold of the arm she'd hurt during the flood and popped it back into place as Erin's scream filled the mine.

"Let's get out of here." Matt grabbed for her hand, but she yanked it away and kept digging.

When a corner of her saddlebag appeared, she turned and grinned at him. "See? I found it." Coughing and gasping for breath, she stepped back. "Would you mind pulling it out?"

Matt knew this was huge. They'd been looking for this stuff for the better part of two weeks, and Erin had found it. They could turn it in, and the police could maybe use it to catch Alex. But he couldn't get past his anger at her. His short-lived relief that she was alive evaporated. Instead, he was infuriated because she'd given him a taste of what it would feel like if she died. And he didn't like the deep ache it had caused in his chest. The sense of loss.

After grabbing the saddlebag, Matt led the way back through the tunnels without another word.

As they approached the entrance, a figure silhouetted in the early morning light stood just outside the mine.

"I knew you could do it, *Eriss*. You just needed the right incentive." Alex backed away. "Throw out the bag, then come out one at a time."

Erin leaned against the mine wall, fished her phone from her pocket and dialed 911. "Damn it! There's no reception inside."

"Think you can manage to pay attention to me this time, and stay here?" Matt whispered to Erin as he dropped the bag next to her. Moving toward the entrance, he called, "Get out of the way, Alex. This ends now."

"Are you sure about that?" Alex grinned as he pulled a knife from his belt, the blade flashing in the pale light.

MATT STEPPED THROUGH the mouth of the mine, ready to stop this guy once and for all. The faint morning light filtered down on Alex, bouncing on the balls of his feet while tossing a knife from hand to hand like some street thug in a dark alley.

"That the same knife you used to kill Hank?" Matt moved farther into the clearing as he spoke, giving himself more room to maneuver.

"The old guy had more muscle than I figured. Had to sharpen it after I gutted him." Alex held the blade up between them, his eyes cold, his tone taunting.

"Drop the knife." Matt's hand drifted close to his holstered gun as he took a step forward. "You're done harassing Erin. Done threatening and killing her friends."

"You think *you're* going to stop me?" Alex's laugh infuriated Matt.

But before he could respond, Alex lunged. Matt stepped to the side and grabbed Alex's arm, twisting it backward, forcing him to let go of the knife. Alex drove his shoulder into Matt's chest and they fell to the ground, Matt struggling to suck in air beneath Alex's weight. He rolled to the side just as Alex's punch grazed his cheek.

They scrambled to their feet, circling each other like wrestlers inside a ring. Alex feinted to the left, then came back with a right cross. Matt blocked the first blow, then took a savage hit to his gut, doubling over in pain. He got even with an uppercut that snapped Alex's head back, then followed with a jab that sent blood spraying from the felon's nose.

But that didn't stop Townsend, who slammed into Matt, driving him into the wall of the mine. Fists flew, Matt's knuckles split against Alex's jaw, but a sharp jab to his ribs left him gasping.

While Alex rained punches into his side, Matt used his superior strength to push him back. They tumbled to the ground again, battling for control. Alex managed to grab Matt's gun from its holster, but Matt yanked it from his grip and sent it flying.

He pinned Alex, holding him down and landing blow after blow. Alex twisted beneath Matt, throwing him off-balance, then rolled away and dived for the knife on the ground. Matt cursed under his breath as Alex rose, flashing the blade as he advanced.

"Stop!" Erin's voice rang out, raw and rough. Both men froze. Matt's gaze slid to her, a few feet away and holding his gun. Her hands trembled, but her tone was steady. "Drop the knife, Alex. Right now!"

Alex hesitated, his eyes darting between Matt and Erin, his lips twisting with anger. Matt thought he might charge at her, but then Alex let out an unsettling laugh and threw the knife down.

Matt snatched the gun from Erin and leveled it at Alex. *His* hands didn't tremble. "Don't even think about moving."

Alex raised his hands, expressions flickering across his face. Anger. Failure. Maybe regret?

Behind them, Erin already held her phone. "I'm calling the police."

Matt kept the gun trained on Alex as he tried to catch his breath, his ribs throbbing with every inhale. Seconds stretched into minutes before the welcome sound of sirens wailed in the distance. Only then did Matt spare a quick glance at Erin.

"Good work," he said in a soft tone.

"Even though I didn't *stay*, as you ordered me to?" She stared at him, her face a blank canvas. As if she'd packed away her emotions and wouldn't need them again anytime soon.

"IT MUST BE a slow crime day in Winston." Erin's throat ached with each word as she counted police cruisers parked along the dirt road near the mine.

"Every day's a slow crime day in Winston." Officer Steve Folsom arched a brow. "Except the ones when *you're* involved."

Erin had gone to school with Steve and knew him well enough to take his teasing in stride. He'd been assigned to stay with her until Detective Martinez took her statement. She followed his eyes across the clearing to where Martinez stood next to Alex, reading him the Miranda warning from a card she held.

"She's not taking any chances with this guy," he said. "Usually Martinez just recites Miranda from memory."

"Bless her for dotting all the *i*'s and crossing all the *t*'s to make sure he stays locked up for the rest of his life." An image of Hank flashed in Erin's mind. "He deserves everything he gets."

"So, you really found the stuff y'all stole?" Steve

asked, then dropped his gaze when Erin scowled at him. "Sorry. I'm just impressed."

Holding the saddlebag tight against her chest with her good arm, she nodded. "It's right here, and I'm not letting go until I hand it to Martinez directly." She leaned toward him. "You know, chain of custody and all that."

"Don't suppose I could just take a quick peek?"

"Not a chance." Erin tightened her grip on the bag as she watched Matt talk to another police officer near the back of an ambulance. "I hope they know he's not going to let them transport him to the hospital in that thing."

As if on the same wavelength, Matt looked across the clearing at her. Maybe he didn't smile at her because his battered face hurt too much. Maybe he didn't raise a hand to wave because his bruised ribs wouldn't allow it. Or maybe he was as mad at her as she was at him. Whatever the reason, he just stared at her for a moment, then turned his attention back to the officer.

"Here comes Martinez." Steve straightened, and Erin wondered if he hoped to move up the ranks to detective someday.

"Ms. Montgomery." The detective nodded. "Quite the week you're having."

"I could have done without it, but you know what they say. All's well—"

"Yes. I do know." Flipping open her notebook, Martinez sighed. "Let's just do a quick rundown of the day to make sure your story matches your friend's over there." She tipped her head toward Matt. "We'll save the long version for your statement at the station later, after you've been checked out at the hospital."

"Oh." Erin looked toward Shadow. "I rode my horse here this morning, and—"

"Officer Folsom here can get the horse back to your ranch. You sound like a bass singer who's gargling with rocks." Martinez raised one brow. "And every time you cough, I could swear I see a puff of dust come out."

The detective couldn't be much older than Erin, but Martinez's matter-of-fact manner intimidated her. Hopefully, she'd intimidate Alex even more.

"Why don't you tell me how all this happened." She raised a hand and gestured around her.

Beginning with Tommy's ring, Erin gave the detective a condensed version of the past twenty-four hours, minimizing the argument with Matt.

With her head still bent over her notepad, Martinez raised her eyes and met Erin's gaze. "And that's the *loot*, as you call it?" she asked, indicating the saddlebag.

"Yes. I wanted to give it to you myself. For chain of custody." Erin held it out. "I've got Tommy's ring and the earring I found in the woods in my pocket. I'm not positive they're part of it, but I figured you, or forensics, or whoever, could check them against the list." For the life of her, she couldn't seem to stop talking.

"Right." Martinez took the saddlebag, unfastened its strap to peer inside, then closed it back up before holding out her hand, palm up.

It took Erin a moment to realize she was waiting for the other two items. After placing them in her hand, she said, "If the ring isn't part of it, I promised Tommy he'd get it back."

Martinez gave her a deadpan look, did an about-face

and started toward the bustle of police activity. She called back over her shoulder, "Oh yeah, don't leave town."

"I won't. Wait. What?" Erin looked to Steve, who fought a losing battle with a laugh. "Why did she tell me to stay in town?"

"Calm down. She's pulling your leg." Steve patted her shoulder. "Martinez is an acquired taste, but she's a brilliant investigator. You're lucky she wasn't a detective ten years ago, when, you know, you—"

"Yes, Steve. I know," Erin said, taking a page from the brilliant detective's playbook and cutting him off. She loosened Shadow's reins from the branch and handed them to him. "See you at the station."

She crossed the clearing to the ambulance and approached Matt with a smile. "How are you feeling?"

"I'll live. You?" Exhaustion replaced any warmth in his tone.

"I have to get checked out at the hospital, but I'm okay." Erin paused, the conversation starting out more awkward than she'd hoped. "By the way, thank you for saving my life in there." She tipped her head toward the mine.

"Just doing my job. No matter how hard you made it." He perched on the back of the ambulance, grimacing with the movement.

"I'm sorry, Matt. I had no way of knowing Alex would show up here. But now it's done. He's been arrested, and we recovered the stolen jewelry." She shrugged her good shoulder. "At least I was right about where it was."

"Well, so long as you were right, that's all that matters."

Erin's head snapped back as if he'd slapped her. "No, what matters is you never believe I'm right about anything until after the fact, when it's too late. You didn't listen to me about the ravine, and I almost died. If you'd listened to me about the mine and come with me, maybe neither one of us would have been hurt."

Matt shook his head. "If you'd listened to me and stayed home, *definitely* neither of us would've been hurt."

He just doesn't get it. "And Alex would still be on the loose, threatening people I care about. Maybe worse." Erin blew out a frustrated breath. "He'd already threatened or killed everyone else in my life he could get to. You were the only one left. I went after the jewelry because I didn't want him hurting you."

Matt closed his eyes for a moment before replying in a softer voice. "I appreciate that, but it was my job to keep you safe, not the other way around. All you had to do was follow my rules, but right up to the end, you refused to do that."

"Well, I hope you and your rules live happily ever after together." Erin leaned toward him and lowered her voice, but it held a bitter edge. "Because if I had followed that last rule of yours, your order to stay in the mine, you might not have a future to look forward to. But hey, no need to thank *me* for saving *your* life."

She walked off toward the second ambulance, blinking the sudden dampness from her eyes. Because Erin Montgomery didn't cry, damn it. Especially not over some control-freak bodyguard who refused to acknowledge her worth.

Chapter Sixteen

The day after Alex's arrest, Matt eased his truck up to the Montgomerys' front gate and buzzed the intercom. Yesterday had dragged on endlessly, and this was the first chance he'd had to swing by and pick up his belongings.

He pressed the buzzer again, but there was no response.

He'd refused the ambulance ride from the mine only by promising the paramedics that he'd drive himself straight to the hospital from the crime scene. And as much as he despised hospitals, it had been the right call. One cracked rib. A deep gash in his cheek that needed stitches. A bruised kidney that still ached with every step.

Hours later, when the emergency room doctor finally released him, Matt had made good on his word to swing by the police station and give them the full version of his statement. By the time he'd finished that, he barely had enough energy to drive to his apartment, climb the stairs and collapse face-first onto his bed.

True, Erin's place was closer than Resolute. But the way things had ended between them at the crime site, he'd been confident she wouldn't let him in to spend the night. Even on the air bed.

Giving up on the intercom, Matt punched in the gate's security code, let himself onto the property and parked near the bunkhouse. He climbed out, grimacing as his ribs protested every movement.

He needed to grab his duffel bag and go. But a stubborn part he couldn't shake hoped to see Erin before he left. He should have kept his mouth shut at the mine. Anger and worry had consumed him when he found Erin gone yesterday morning. She'd betrayed his trust again, put herself in danger and still seemed only to care that her hunch about the loot was right.

He regretted not keeping his reactions under control. Some of what she'd said had been valid but hit too close to the truth, and he'd made things between them even worse by holding his ground. And now he honestly wasn't sure where his emotions lay. Thirty-six hours ago, Matt would have bet every surfboard he owned that he and Erin would make it long term. And though he still wanted to be with her, that old reliable voice in his head urged him to run without looking back.

He knocked on the bunkhouse door, wincing when his raw knuckles hit the wood.

Again, no response.

"I'm coming in," he called out.

Still no answer, so he unlocked the door and stepped inside.

Everything looked exactly the same.

Matt scoffed at himself.

Of course it does. It's only been one day.

But it felt longer. It felt permanent. As if he were trespassing where he no longer belonged. A heavy shadow settled over his heart.

He headed into the junk room. The air mattress sat in a corner, deflated, the pump next to it.

She had wasted no time erasing him from her life.

He packed his clothes into his duffel, and by the time he walked out of the room, nothing remained to show he'd ever been there.

Except now, it was all organized.

A dry chuckle escaped him, one tinged with irony. He remembered his first day here and how Erin had made it clear she wanted him gone. Well, now he was going.

He pulled the front door closed behind him, making sure the lock clicked. Glancing at the security cameras mounted on the house and barn, he made a mental note to have Nate check with Erin about keeping them. And to remind her to reset the code combinations for the whole ranch.

Almost at the front gate, he caught a glimpse of movement in his side mirror. A figure on horseback. His heart hammering, Matt braked and twisted around in his seat to peer through the truck's back window.

Erin sat astride Shadow, her back straight and tall. Her gaze met his across the distance, felt more than seen.

She didn't ride toward him. She didn't wave.

Instead, she guided Shadow around and rode away, her silhouette fading into the landscape.

Matt gripped the steering wheel, his raw knuckles turning white. He fought the urge to turn the truck back and go after her.

She'd made her choice.

R EDEMPTION PRANCED ACROSS the corral, no hint of a limp in his step.

"Good boy." Erin slipped him a piece of carrot. "I think it's time for you to go home."

She glanced at her watch and noticed the day of the week. Monday. A violent shudder wracked her body.

Today was the deadline. Two weeks ago, almost to the hour, Alex Townsend began his reign of destruction. Erin's eyes drifted to the spot where Hank's body had lain, her mind only too willing to manufacture the pools of blood staining the earth around him. How much more devastation would Alex have wreaked by now if he hadn't been arrested?

Shrugging off these morose thoughts that had settled over her like a shroud, Erin led Redemption to the barn. Although glad the horse had recovered from his injury, she would miss him. His workouts helped fill the empty hours she faced now that Matt had left. After grooming the gelding and moving him into his stall, she brought out Blaze.

"It's your turn to lead today, you beauty." Erin brushed the mare, then saddled her for riding. After opening Shadow's stall, she clicked her tongue to bring her out. "And you get to run free this time."

When she exercised both horses by herself, Erin rode one and had the other follow alongside. She'd trained Blaze and Shadow well enough to not worry about either one running off on their own.

The late morning sky was clear, the air frigid enough to see the horses' plumes of breath each time they exhaled. They'd get a good run in when they reached the meadow. But they walked in the meantime, Erin in no hurry to end this part of her day. Her animals brought her comfort.

Erin's mother's call, perfectly timed to come through after all the Alex furor had ended, brought excellent news. Her dad had extended his business. Erin would have the whole ranch to herself without having to answer to dear old Mom. But for the first time in her life, she experienced loneliness, not simply solitude. Without Matt around, and without the nonstop activity of the past two weeks, she didn't know what to do with herself.

I was fine before him, and I'm fine now.

It angered her that she even cared he was gone. He hadn't trusted her to make a good decision. He'd been angry that she followed her gut and wound up being right. He hadn't even said goodbye when he left. With a heavy, aching heart, her choice to turn away had been her only recourse to avoid more pain.

When they reached the meadow, the horses took off at a gallop, their hooves thundering across the ground. Erin's discontent lifted away, and she intended to let it stay gone. She had trusted herself and been right to do so. The time had arrived to make more life-changing decisions on her own. She didn't need her mother's constant disapproval. She didn't need to lean on Matt, or any man, for support.

Although the path to the future was still unclear, the destination wasn't.

Erin's equine therapy ranch would happen.

Chapter Seventeen

After adjusting her attitude about herself, her plans and life in general, Erin enjoyed two more months of freedom before her parents returned. Their extended trip translated to a grand tour of Europe, Asia and parts of the Middle East. Combining business and pleasure had always been a sound financial tactic for her dad. And the very few phone calls home meant her mom had planned the itinerary and was too busy enjoying herself to worry about the ranch.

All good news for Erin. And the recent meeting she'd had with the family attorney had left her downright euphoric.

But now, she meandered around the main house, waiting for her parents to arrive home from the airport so she could greet them. As was expected of her. Her stomach roiled in anticipation of what she thought of as *THE CONVERSATION*. Inhaling deep breaths, she trailed her fingers along the mantel, not surprised to find it dusted and polished. The Montgomerys' housekeeper hadn't slacked off for a moment, even with her parents on the other side of the world.

An engine purred in the circular drive out front, and car doors opened and closed. Erin shook out her arms to release her nerves, pulled her mouth into a loving smile and opened the door.

"Erin, darling." Her mother entered the house, air-kissed her daughter and left her in a cloud of perfume. "Have you lost weight? You're so thin."

"Hi, Dad." Erin hugged her father as he came through the door.

"You look wonderful," he whispered in her ear.

"No, Mother, I haven't lost weight." She opened the door wider for the driver, who struggled to haul what looked like twice the luggage her parents had left with into the house.

"We had the most wonderful time. It was a shame you didn't join us." Her mother took off a fashionable coat Erin had never seen before and draped it over a chair. "Especially considering all that ugly business going on here."

"Why don't you tell me about your trip." Now that she was face-to-face with her mom, Erin needed some time to gather her nerve about her own news. "Where did you go? What did you see?"

"Oh, where didn't we go?" Her mother settled on the couch, shooting a glare at her father as he fled to his office. "After we left Paris, we went to Japan. You know I've always wanted to go there, and it was as amazing as…"

Sitting in a nearby chair, Erin only half listened while her mom recounted every city in every country they'd visited, every purchase in every store she'd made and every delectable morsel from every restaurant that passed her lips. What she did hear sounded like it had been an incredible trip.

Meanwhile, the other half of her brain rehearsed the already memorized speech planned for her mom. And as had become her habit during all the years of squabbling with her mother in her head, she'd also prepared her mother's side of *THE CONVERSATION*. For every argument her mother would make, Erin had a counter. For every reason why not, Erin had a reason why. For every threat, emotional plea and criticism, Erin had a spine of steel and she wasn't afraid to use it.

As soon as she gathered her damn nerve.

"...but your father decided it was time to come home, so here we are."

"Wow."

"Now tell me what you've been up to. But before you start, I heard about all that nasty business at that old mine, and I'm going to give that security company a piece of my mind." She crossed the room to the bar cart and poured herself a sherry. "Would you like one, dear?"

"No thanks. I'm fine."

Returning to the couch, her mom continued, "That bodyguard they sent out here, Mark, Mike, whatever his name is, had no right to put you in such danger. And poor Hank, getting killed like that."

"His name is Matt, and he never put me in danger, Mom. He kept me safe while he was here." Erin's thoughts drifted to the hunter's cabin during the storm. If only her mother knew about that and the flood. "I was the one who decided to go to the mine. Matt didn't want me to."

Her mother paused, sherry glass an inch away from her mouth. "*You* decided to go. Now, why doesn't that surprise me? Your father and I spent a great deal of money for your protection, and you just go chasing after that... that *criminal* on your own." She tossed back her sherry and set the glass on the end table next to her. "Good grief,

Erin. You're almost thirty years old, and you still don't have the sense God gave a goose."

Wait...wait... Yes, there it is.

It seemed Erin's nerve just needed a slight nudge from her anger.

"I had enough sense to want to make things right." Erin rose and paced around the room as she spoke. "I went to the mine, I recovered all the stolen jewelry from the robbery. Matt subdued and held Alex until the police arrived and took him into custody."

"You never should have—"

"For the first time in ten years, I trusted a man. And it was the right call." Erin stopped in front of her mom. "For the first time in ten years, I trusted myself, and it was the right call. I do have good instincts. And if I put myself in danger, it was a risk I was willing to take to make up for my past mistakes. It was my choice, and I don't care what you or Matt or anyone else thinks about it."

Her mother stood, refusing to meet Erin's gaze. "Well, I'm exhausted from traveling. I think I'll go freshen up."

"That's not all, Mom." She waited her mother out, until she looked Erin in the eye. "Hank left everything he owned to me. I won't bore you with the details, but because he set everything up in advance, the attorney is already probating the will."

"What exactly do you mean by 'set everything up'?"

"I mean his property will become an equine therapy ranch." Erin watched her mother drop onto the couch. "He knew my dream was to use horses to help people deal with mental or physical challenges."

"That's ridiculous." Her mother held out her glass to Erin. "Would you please bring me a refill, dear?"

Erin rolled her eyes but did as she was asked.

"That will never work, Erin. I'm sure you don't have the necessary education for something like that."

"You know darn well my bachelor's degree is in veterinarian technology. I have plenty of certifications to work with horses. But I'll hire an actual therapist, and who knows? Maybe I'll go back to school for my master's, maybe even my doctorate."

Her mother almost snorted sherry out of her nose. "How do you plan to pay for all that?"

This was where Erin's plan to be self-sufficient ran into a hitch.

"Since you control Grandma's trust—"

"Those payments don't start until you turn thirty."

"But she told me she'd specified certain circumstances under which money could be released early. I believe starting my own business qualifies as one of her exceptions."

"Early release of any money from that trust would be at my discretion. And I'm certainly not doing it for some silly pipe dream that will never get off the ground." She set her glass on the table and stood. "Besides, we need you here to work with our dressage clients."

Erin's gut churned with anxiety, but she straightened her spine and met her mother's gaze. "I am moving to Hank's property, and I will be turning it into a therapy ranch. It's time for me to take control of my own life."

"Then you'll be doing it on a shoestring budget, dear, because the trust is locked for another two years." Her mother's brows struggled toward a frown, but the latest round of Botox injections won out. "Although I don't approve of this, when you're finally ready to face reality, we'll welcome you home again. Just like we did the last time you exercised such poor judgment." She turned away and, without another word, went upstairs.

Although Erin had trudged to the main house, dreading with every step the talk with her mother, she seemed to almost float above the ground during the return trip to the bunkhouse. As if she'd removed the proverbial millstone from around her neck that she had carried for the past ten years.

A range of emotions as wide as Texas itself tumbled through her, and she tried to focus only on the positive ones. Relief, excitement and self-confidence topped the list. Disappointment in her mother's attitude toward Erin and her plans hurt, but not as much as she'd expected. She pushed that one away. When she did, two more rolled into its spot. Sadness. Regret. They merged to form an image in her mind.

Matt Franklin's face.

Chapter Eighteen

After finishing up two jobs near Austin, Matt met Nate at the Busy B Café in Resolute.

"I emailed you my report this morning." Matt took a bite of his burger and chewed slowly, savoring the flavor.

Nate nodded. "I got it. Sounds like these last two assignments were your easiest of the year so far."

"Considering the Montgomery job was the only other one, that's not saying much." He shifted in his seat, wincing at the residual pain in his ribs.

"It's been a few months. Shouldn't you be all healed up by now?" Nate drained his coffee cup and held it up in Marge's direction.

"You would think. At least the ER doctor's teeny, tiny stitches in my face maintained my rugged boyish charm." He laughed when Nate almost choked on a french fry.

Marge, the owner of the diner, worked her way to their table, her orthopedic shoes squeaking across the linoleum floor. "You boys need refills?" She held up the carafe of coffee she'd brought with her.

After filling both cups, she leaned in close to Matt's face, squinting. "I can barely tell where that big old cut was." She straightened. "Must have been a plastic surgeon wannabe who stitched you up."

Matt smiled at Nate and spread his arms wide. "What'd I tell you?" He looked up at Marge. "Do I still have my rugged, boyish charm?"

"Sure you do." The older woman patted him on the shoulder. "And just enough of it to woo that Erin Montgomery and take her off the market before some other charming boy snags her."

Matt glanced at Nate, who stayed quiet while he dipped a fry in ketchup.

"I'm not so sure Ms. Montgomery wants to be taken off the market." Matt shifted again, now uncomfortable *and* feeling awkward.

"And I'm not so sure discussing women being on or off the market is socially acceptable these days." Nate shrugged.

Marge glared at Nate. "It's my diner, and I'll talk any way I want to." She then turned to Matt. "I heard tell you two had something going on while you were protecting her. If you ask me, you should figure out why you don't anymore, fix it and get it going again."

"Thanks for the advice." Eager to change the subject, Matt added, "And these are the best burgers west of the Pecos."

Marge and Nate looked at each other, then burst out laughing.

"I appreciate that, honey. But when you look like one of them surfers from California, trying to talk like a Texan just don't work." She leaned in again and stage-whispered, "And we're east of the Pecos. Not west."

She squeaked off toward the kitchen, laughing and muttering, "West of the Pecos. Don't that beat all?"

Nate held his napkin to his mouth to hide his chuckles.

"Whatever." Matt shrugged it off and took another bite of his burger. "At least I tried."

"Check a map next time." Nate leaned back against his bench seat. "You know, Marge might not be wrong."

"This from the man whose company motto is don't fall in love with the client?"

"You can't put that toothpaste back in the tube." Nate arched a brow.

Concentrating on his condiments, Matt said, "How'd you figure it out?"

"Give me some credit." Nate snorted. "And you haven't been yourself since the job ended. What happened between you two?"

"Well, we got caught in the storm—"

"Not that part. What happened that you're not even talking to each other?"

Matt thought about it before answering. "I was more concerned with my rules than listening to Erin's opinions. I guess I should have done a better job of balancing the two." He popped another fry in his mouth. "But what's done is done, and she made it clear I've lost my chance with her."

"I know this is the opposite of what I usually say, but you shouldn't give up on her so quickly. I almost made that mistake myself with Sara, and I'm really glad I came to my senses in time." Nate nodded, as if agreeing with himself that he'd done the right thing. "Maybe it's not too late for you and Erin."

Matt shrugged but didn't reply. He wished Nate was right, but at this point, that was another decision Erin would have to make.

"I do have some good news." Nate grinned. "Winston

PD is processing the reward, and you should have the money any day."

"That's nice," Matt mumbled, still thinking about Erin.

"Nice? It's enough to buy back in as a partner."

Matt perked up at that. "Seriously? But shouldn't it go to Erin? Technically, she's the one who recovered the jewelry."

"She's not eligible for it because she was involved in the original crime." Still smiling, Nate added, "Plus, she made it clear, even if she were eligible, she wouldn't take a dime."

Matt tried to ignore his guilt about the way he'd ended things with Erin. "So, you and me—we're partners again?" He lifted his water glass and waited for Nate to clink his against it.

"To partners."

"This is the best news I've had since I moved to Texas." Matt couldn't wipe the grin off his face. He would finally share ownership of *their* company with his best friend again.

"Scooch over." Charlie, the bodyguard who had stayed with Maeve O'Roarke, dropped into the booth next to Nate while Gabe forced his muscled self in on Matt's side. "What's this confab about?"

"Matt's buying into the company as an equal partner," Nate said.

"Oh, man. We're gonna have two bosses now?" Charlie rolled her eyes.

"It was bad enough with just the one." Gabe stared at Nate with a straight face.

Matt could never tell when the big man was joking. "Yeah? Well, get used to it." He elbowed Gabe in the side.

"Just kidding, Matt. I'm glad you did it so quickly," Charlie said, then kicked her Southern drawl up a notch. "Y'all goin' to the barn raisin'?" Her eyes twinkled.

"What barn raising?" Matt asked.

"The horse therapy ranch." Charlie widened her eyes in surprise at Matt. "Figured you'd know all about it, since she was your girlfri... Ouch, why'd you kick me?" She glared at Nate.

"I was going to tell Matt about it." Nate fortified himself with more coffee. "Erin inherited Hank's property, and she's turning it into a therapy ranch. But the place needs a lot of work, and rumor has it Erin's mom won't release any of her trust money early. So some businesses in Winston are donating supplies, and we're all going to build her a new barn and whatever else we can."

"She still won't be able to open anytime soon," Charlie said. "She'll need to buy horses and hire a therapist and a bunch of other stuff. But at least the property will be ready."

"We're all going, and my sister and brothers and their spouses will be there." Nate avoided Matt's eyes.

"When is it?" Matt asked.

"Beginning of the month." Gabe glanced at Charlie. "Are we eating here or what?"

"Hold your horses. Marge is heading this way." Charlie flashed her dazzling smile at Marge.

Gabe grumbled about needing sustenance.

And Matt realized he had no one to blame but himself for being out of the loop when it came to Erin and her new ranch.

But maybe it wasn't too late to help.

Chapter Nineteen

The first Saturday of June dawned cooler than everyone had expected—welcome news for the passel of friends and strangers who'd volunteered for the grueling work of a barn raising for Tranquil Trails Equine Therapy Ranch. Matt parked his truck and walked across grass damp with early morning dew, the last of the ground mist swirling as he passed. Long into his sleepless night, he'd debated the wisdom of coming here today. But like that moth to a flame, he craved nearness to Erin.

Maybe I am a chump after all.

Sure, he was gratified to play a part in her dream. What she was trying to accomplish was admirable and would help a lot of people. But to be so close to her and not tease her, laugh with her, touch her would be torture. His version of the moth's death from the light that attracted it.

The sight of the Montgomery Ranch foreman directing volunteers surprised Matt. "Morning. Erin's mother okay with you being here?"

The man chortled. "Hell no, but they have no say about what I do during my day off. She okay with you being here?" he asked with a wink.

Matt grinned. "I expect she wouldn't be, but I don't work for her anymore."

"Figured as much, what with that creep out of the picture. But, you know, after you and Erin... Well, I flat out didn't expect to see you here either."

Matt gave him a small, one-shoulder shrug. "Worthy cause."

"A very worthy cause," the foreman said with another wink, and Matt knew he wasn't referring to the ranch.

Given the job of directing supply trucks just arriving, he waved his arms to direct one loaded with tools and a second, longer flatbed piled high with donated boards and posts to the spot where the builders waited.

Once they'd parked, he greeted each truck driver with a handshake, and introductions were made before the real work of unloading began. The aroma of freshly cut lumber reminded Matt of the times he'd spent in the woods with Erin. A warm, earthy scent that he found pleasing.

Not that he found much to be pleased about these days.

And whose fault is that?

After the trucks were emptied, Matt spied his boss. He headed toward Nate and Nate's very *un*identical twin, Noah, and the three began laying wood studs on a framing table, measuring the wall studs according to blueprint specs, then sawing them to length.

"Slow down, Noah," Nate said. "Measure twice, cut once."

Noah inhaled. "I was distracted. The smell of those grills warming up is making my mouth water." He turned to Matt. "Our brother, Adam, is the best home chef in the county, and he excels at grilling."

"You and your stomach," Nate grumbled. "It's dawn, you blockhead. Hours before lunch. How can you already be thinking about food?"

Matt laid a stud on the table, and Nate redirected his attention. "Wait, Matt. Not like that. Here, let me show you."

Clearly, the Reed brothers had more construction know-how than Matt, but he was always willing to learn. *Like horseback riding.*

He swore under his breath. Why did every action, every thought, always circle back around to Erin?

"Stop harping on the man," Noah said. "Anyone can see we got us a city boy here."

Nate nodded. "A useless city boy."

Matt's brows shot up. "You clowns work that out ahead of time?"

They grinned, and Matt got an inkling of what they must have been like as kids. "You're on your own. I'm going to take my city-boy ways and help elsewhere."

He walked away to the sound of their laughter. The Reeds were like that. The twins, Cassie, Adam, even their spouses. If they didn't tease you, they didn't care about you. At least, that's what Matt kept telling himself.

As he made his way to the slab for the new barn, he noticed vehicles now lined both sides of the state road for a half mile or more, parked on the shoulders along the Montgomerys' property and Hank's—no, Erin's—property. Hank would have loved this.

Over near Hank's old, small barn, scores of people moved about like ants at a picnic, issuing directions, offering advice or just chatting. Children ran around, squealing and laughing. Women shooed them away while working under pitched canopies, organizing a water station, first aid station and a food station. Hammers pounded, saws buzzed. A day of organized chaos with an atmosphere of raucous anticipation.

When the Reeds showed up for an event, apparently they brought the entire town of Resolute with them. To be fair, Winston's townsfolk were nearly as plentiful. Matt surveyed the spectacle. All of this, the planning, donations, supplies and people, were here for one reason—to help Erin realize her dream of opening a therapy horse ranch. The turnout was beyond amazing. Matt thought back to his own childhood and wondered how different his life might have been if there had been a place like this for him.

A pang of envy shot through him. He was tired of not belonging. To a community. To someone.

To Erin.

His chest burned with a stabbing ache, one that happened frequently these days. He did his best to ignore it, but fools deserved what they got.

Charlie appeared to be in charge of the barn construction, so Matt headed for her. Tall and well-muscled, she'd tied her blond hair in a ponytail that hung through the back of a gimme cap with Resolute Security's logo. She wore a sleeveless T-shirt under overalls and old work boots, yet she somehow managed to make all that look feminine.

"Put me to work," Matt said.

She tugged a bandanna from her back pocket and blotted the sweat on her forehead. "Luke had to bail. Got called out on a case. But you can help Gabe." She shoved the bandanna back into her pocket. "I was happy to see the foundation already set. Nice job, that."

Matt saw nothing but an ordinary concrete slab.

Whether it was a nice job or not, he had no idea. "So, you know about this stuff?"

"I've spent a lot of my vacations building homes for a charity organization, so yeah, I know a bit."

"Well, look at you, you big softy."

"Tell anyone and I'll have to take you out."

Matt held up two fingers in promise. "To the grave," he said, grinning. As a woman in a male-dominated field, Charlie worked hard to prove she was one of the best. And she was.

"Grab a two-by-six," she said, pointing to the stack of lumber. "Take it over to Gabe. He'll tell you what to do."

"You got it, boss."

He started to turn away when Charlie grabbed his arm and stopped him. "Listen, I wasn't going to say anything, but the hell with it."

"Mind telling me what you're talking about?" But he figured he already knew.

"I heard what you did. Giving up your shot at becoming *my* boss."

Matt's jaw clenched.

"Look, I'm not going to tell anyone. I know you want the donation to be anonymous and all. But I want you to know that gifting Erin that reward money is pretty awesome."

"Not very anonymous if you know about it. How'd you find out? Nate?"

"Indirectly. I accidentally overheard him talking to his wife about it."

Matt grunted, turned to go and stumbled, nearly doing a face-plant before regaining his balance. He looked down. "Whoa there!" Tangled up in his legs was young Tommy.

"Sorry, Mr. Matt. Glad you didn't fall. Gotta go." The boy dashed off, several children chasing him down in a mean game of tag.

"This is a dangerous place," Gabe said, coming up to them to grab more lumber. "Matt, quit lollygagging with this pretty lady and get to work."

Matt winked at Charlie, picked up a wooden stud and followed Gabe. "Lollygagging?"

"Don't judge. That PI we use turned me on to word-of-the-day calendars."

For several hours, Matt, alongside Gabe, members of the Winston police force and dozens of other volunteers, lifted and hammered together the barn's frame. Others worked on the trusses for the roof before lunatics with no fear of heights laid down the metal roofing sheets.

Throughout the day, Matt kept constant tabs on Erin as she flitted from place to place, speaking with everyone, it seemed. Everyone but him. He made sure to steer clear of her. It was one thing to lend a helping hand, it was another to let their personal stuff ruin her day.

"Lunch break, everyone!" Charlie shouted, and the hungry group of workers dropped their tools and stampeded toward the live oaks shading a grouping of picnic tables and benches.

Long tables were piled high with food. Potluck dishes of every type—casseroles, salads, rolls, sandwiches, plus all the fixings to go with Adam Reed's burgers and hot dogs. Marge, the owner of the Busy B Café, presided over the array like a sergeant major.

"Now, Bill, you go on and leave some of that pie for other folks."

"Yes, ma'am. It just looks so darn good."

"Well, of course it's good. I baked it. And watch that language. There are children about," she scolded. "Jace! Goodness me. Use the serving thongs and not your grimy fingers, if you please."

"Sorry, Ms. Marge. Real sorry."

"Why, Annabelle Gibson, you look rail thin. Take a second helping."

"Oh, no thank you. I'm full."

"Fiddlesticks. Here, you take this, and you eat it. You hear me?"

"Marge is a real force of nature, isn't she?" Erin, sweaty and disheveled and never more beautiful to him, moved along the other side of the table, casually scooping food onto her plate as if nothing had ever passed between them.

How had he let everything go so wrong?

Matt gritted his teeth. "She is that."

"I didn't expect to see you here." Her voice was soft, enticing, a siren's song making his nerves crackle.

Hoping he appeared indifferent, he shrugged. "Resolute Security is a donor. The boss wanted us here."

"Oh, I see. Makes sense."

Was that disappointment he heard? Or was his wishful thinking working overtime? He plopped a spoonful of something onto his plate. He didn't know what. Didn't really care. "It's a good cause. I would have come anyway."

"Well, thank you." Having reached the end of the table, her plate full, she said, "Take care, Matt."

And that was that. Whatever had been between them was over. He was certain now.

She turned and walked away, taking his heart with her.

No second chance for him. Irony was a vindictive shrew.

AFTER LUNCH, ERIN LED a group of volunteers to what would become the training paddocks. Never in her wildest dreams could she have imagined such an outpouring of support. A perfect reason to smile. And yet, her smile felt brittle and phony on the outside, while she felt miserable on the inside.

Matt didn't love her. He'd made that plain enough. She wondered if he'd ever cared about her. It seemed impossible that she had misjudged the situation so completely. Again. But the evidence told her otherwise. What twisted irony that just when she'd decided to trust herself, Matt blindsided her with a sucker punch.

Can't blame Matt. I won't. I'm owning my life, screwups and all.

Growth only came when you learned from your mistakes, and her mistakes were telling her that love was not in the cards for her. At least not with Matt. Love for her would have to come from the gratification she'd find the first time some kid smiled down on her from the back of one of her therapy horses. It was enough. It would have to be.

"Hey, everyone, can I have your attention, please?" she shouted to the landscaping crews. "Team leaders, raise your hands. Great. Team A will be with Marcella over there. You're in charge of pulling weeds. Where's Cruz? There you are. His team, Team B, will be tying up the broken tree limbs. And my group, Team C, will be in charge of clearing brush. Everyone find a team. Don't all bunch up in one place. Spread out evenly between the groups. That's it."

Several minutes passed with people shuffling around before Erin could delineate three relatively evenly populated teams. "Okay, listen up. Whichever group finishes first—"

"Gets dinner on me at my place in Resolute," Adam Reed declared. He smiled at Erin as she mouthed, "Thank you." A much better prize than what she'd planned to hand out.

Charlie, on the brush crew, waved her gimme cap in the air. "Woo-hoo!" she hollered. "Best steaks in the county."

The crowd cheered in approval.

"Come on, team! Let's show these punks what we're made of," Charlie called out, clearly up for the challenge.

Erin laughed. Strange, really, that Charlie was becoming a good friend in such a short time. One bodyguard coming into her life, one going out.

About two hours into the backbreaking contest, Tommy's mother came running up to Erin, her eyes wide, a piece of paper fluttering in her hand. "Erin! Erin!"

"Whoa, slow down, Jill. Is everything okay with Tommy?"

Unable to speak while she caught her breath, Jill nodded in the affirmative while bending at the waist to rest her hands on her knees. Finally, she stood and waved the paper in front of Erin's face. "You're never going to believe this. Look!"

Erin took the sheet. "My bank statement?"

Jill, who worked at the bank in Winston, nodded toward the paper. "Yes. And?"

Erin looked again. "And what?"

Jill folded her arms across her chest, almost as if hugging herself. "Seriously? You don't see it?"

Erin looked for a third time. "Um, no. I don't... What the—" Her head shot up. "Is this a mistake?"

Jill's smile stretched from ear to ear. "I thought so too, at first. So, I checked. Girl, it's not a mistake. That's one hundred percent legit."

The statement showed a deposit into her ranch operating account. A huge deposit, even by Montgomery standards. "Where did this come from?"

"I have no idea. It was tagged as an anonymous donation."

"Mom! Mom! Mom!" Tommy ran up to Jill and wrapped his arms around her legs. "You're here. Finally."

Over the top of Tommy's head, Jill told Erin, "I had to work, so my sister's been keeping an eye on him."

Jill extracted herself from her son's loving embrace. "Say hi to Miss Erin."

"I already did. What's that?" He pointed at the paper she held.

"Just some boring adult stuff," Erin said, still wondering if she was dreaming.

Jill scoffed. "Adult stuff, yes, but boring? Not by half."

Tommy looked from Erin to his mom. "How come?"

Jill squatted until she was face-to-face with him. She thumb-wiped dirt from his cheek. "Because Miss Erin has a secret admirer."

Tommy's nose scrunched up. "Does he want to kiss her? 'Cause that's gross."

"No, he doesn't want to kiss her. He wants her to have money for this horse ranch."

"She should say thank you."

Jill stood and finger-combed his tousled hair. "Yes, well, she would, except she doesn't know who gave her the money."

"I know. It was Mr. Matt."

Both Jill and Erin said, "What?" in unison, startling Tommy.

"It's okay," Jill assured him. "It just surprised us. How do you know that?"

"'Cause I heard him tell that lady over there." Tommy pointed to Charlie.

"What did he say, honey?" Jill asked.

"Um, I don't remember. Can I have a soda?"

"No, you may not. It's bad for your teeth. But I need you to think. What makes you think it was Mr. Matt who gave Erin the money?"

"Mo-om."

"Don't whine, Tommy." Jill looked at Erin and shrugged.

"I know for a fact Matt doesn't have that kind of money," Erin said.

"Oh, oh, oh," Tommy said, jumping up and down. "I remember! The lady," he said, again pointing to Charlie, "said he wasn't going to be her boss and he said so what it was his reward money."

Erin's mind spun. Matt wanted that partnership more than anything. She needed to return it to him somehow.

"Are we done now? Can I go play?"

"Sure, honey," Jill said, and Tommy darted off. "Well?" she asked Erin.

"Well, what?"

Jill gave her a knowing look. "Are you going to talk to him?"

"I am not." Matt had made his feelings, or lack thereof, well known. She'd blindly followed her heart once before, and that ended poorly. No way would she make the same mistake again. She was a stronger person now.

"I have a feeling the donation came from my father," Erin lied. Anything to keep from having to face Matt.

"I think you're being a fool."

"You're wrong about that. This is the least foolish thing I've done in a long while."

Anything more, her heart wouldn't survive.

WHY WAS HE LINGERING? There was no reason to stay, and yet he did. Matt could kick himself. If only he'd tried harder to mend the rift between them, maybe he wouldn't be here now, alone, leaning back against the new paddock fence, one boot braced behind him against the lowest rail.

To the west, the setting sun grazed the horizon, casting the newly completed barn in dark relief. A beautiful scene, solemn and lonely. Time to leave. Past time, if he was being honest.

Just a little bit longer, he told himself. Then he would go.

And yet, his thoughts were so full of Erin laughing at him, defying him, making love with him, that he couldn't bring himself to go.

He was a fool.

ERIN WALKED THROUGH the dim interior of the barn, the smell of new lumber teasing her nose. The volunteers had all left, the day was drawing down and she was enjoying a bit of quiet solitude. She surveyed the barn, marveling at how everything was so new and clean.

A nicker caught her attention, and she wandered over to Shadow's stall. She dropped his head over the Dutch door.

"That's right. Come here, girl." She rubbed the horse's soft nose. "What do you think about your new digs? Nice, isn't it?" Erin made sure there was plenty of hay for the mare to munch on and then wandered over to visit with Blaze.

"Hi there, Blaze. You didn't think I'd forgotten about you, did you? No, I would never do that."

At last, the day's activities began to take their toll. Exhausted, she shuffled over to the main door and prepared to close it up for the night. And gasped. Silhouetted against a sky ablaze with orange and crimson was Matt.

What was he still doing here? She hadn't seen or heard from him in months, and then today he showed up out of the blue to help out. And the donation, what was that all about? She was beyond grateful for it, but if she wasn't good enough for a second chance, why was he doing all this for her? Why didn't he just leave?

"You should talk to him."

Erin whipped around and slapped a hand over her thundering heart. "Jeez, Charlie. You scared the daylights out of me. What are you still doing here?"

"Love you, too."

"Sorry. I didn't mean that the way it sounded."

Charlie grinned. "Yeah, I know, but it's fun messing with you."

"Cute. But really, why are you still here?"

"Just checking the new security system. Once a security nerd, always a security nerd." She nodded in Matt's direction. "Whatcha gonna to do about that?"

"Wait for him to leave?"

"Chicken. Why not just go out there and talk to him?"

"I tried that earlier. It didn't work."

"Seriously? I've never met two more stubborn people." Charlie rubbed her forehead as if she had a momentous headache.

"He doesn't care about me. He's made that perfectly clear. I don't see what we have left to talk about."

"Don't you?"

The donation.

"Do you, um, I mean, what do you…do you know?"

"I'm really hoping you never seek a career in a clandestine service, because you have absolutely no skills ferreting out information."

Erin pointed out the barn. "Clearly, I'm not about to apply for a job at Spies R Us."

Charlie laughed. "Good thing."

"So, what *do* you know?"

"About what?" the bodyguard said with a smirk.

Getting frustrated, Erin said, "You know."

"Do I?"

"You're driving me crazy."

"And you're avoiding."

Erin was, but it was no fun being called out.

"Go on. Talk to him. What could it hurt?"

Charlie didn't understand. Being rejected again would tear Erin apart, shatter her heart. But hey, no big deal. So, like the fool she was, she walked outside.

In the shadows of early dusk, she approached Matt. She

almost turned around, but he'd know she was chicken, just as Charlie had claimed. For that reason alone, she kept going.

She stopped a few feet from where he stood. "Thank you for all the work you did today. I still can't believe the barn and grounds are ready to go."

His voice, when it came, sounded almost like low, masculine music. "I'm glad I could lend a hand. I've got a lot to learn about construction, but I picked up a fair amount today."

Silence. Long and painful.

"Matt, I know you donated your reward money to the ranch."

"Does everyone in Boone County know?" Matt massaged his temples. "How did you find out?"

"Accidentally, but that doesn't matter. I can't let you do it." Erin planted her fists on her hips.

"Too late. It's already done."

"I can't accept it. I'll cut you a check for the full amount on Monday." She dropped her arms. "I appreciate the gesture, but you need that money for your partnership. That's been your dream, and you deserve it."

"It's not a big deal. It'll just take me a bit longer to become a partner."

"I don't understand you."

"Don't you? Can't you see how not being with you is ripping me apart?"

He'd raised his voice, but Erin was in no mood to be cowed. "No, I don't see! All I know is you can barely stand the sight of me."

"What the hell are you talking about?"

"Ever since the mine, you won't look at me except with

a glare. You won't talk to me. And oh, yeah, you left without bothering to say goodbye. Was anything between us real, or was it all for the job?"

His voice lowered again, Matt said, "Everything I've done since the day I met you was to keep you safe."

"So it *was* all for your job."

Matt swiped his hand through his hair, leaving it standing on end. "When I thought I'd lost you in the cave-in, I died on the inside. I've never protected anyone like I did you, but it was more than that."

"Why? Help me understand."

"Can't you see? I love you, Erin Montgomery. Didn't want to. Tried not to. But I do. And nothing you say or do will ever change that."

"Even if I refuse to follow your rules?" She cocked one brow.

"Even then."

"Even if I think I'm right and you're wrong?" The other brow rose.

"I doubt that would happen, but even then." The corner of his mouth kicked up in a smile.

"Then why would I ever want to change that? I love you, too, Matt Franklin."

He curved one hand behind her neck and kissed her until she couldn't breathe.

Panting, Erin took Matt's hand in hers. "Come on. Let's ride the property."

ERIN AND MATT worked side by side in Hank's old barn, saddling her two horses she'd brought with her. She glanced across Shadow's back at him, a small smile tugging at the corners of her mouth.

"What?" he asked.

But her days of teasing Matt about his fear of horses or lack of knowledge were behind them. These days, he knew as well as Erin how to groom, saddle, mount and ride. He may not be quite as good as or as fast, but he knew how. He'd learned during the short time he lived with her, and he hadn't forgotten a thing.

"Nothing." But she widened her smile just because it would irritate him.

Once the horses were ready, they mounted and set off at a leisurely pace next to each other.

"All of the buildings and operating areas are near the barn. I want to show you the rest of it, the fields, the wild parts," Erin said. "It's a tiny fraction of the size of my parents' ranch, but it's plenty big enough for what I want to do, even if I get more horses down the road."

They rode in comfortable silence through pastures dotted with wildflowers and huge trees that provided shade. When the horses picked their way across a stream, Matt asked, "Is this the same one that runs across the Montgomery Ranch?"

"Yep." She gave him a mischievous grin. "Don't tell my mother. She might find a way to dam it up if she found out."

Matt laughed.

Crossing through more fields, he said, "Every acre of this place feels like you."

Erin glanced at him. "That's the plan. Make it mine. It already feels like it is."

The air was warm, carrying the faint scent of earth and grass, mingled with the subtle sweetness of blossoms.

Erin brought Shadow to a stop at the edge of a large

field. She dismounted and waited for Matt to do the same. When he landed on two feet with no hopping around, she smiled.

"Come on. This is my favorite spot. We'll tie up the horses here."

After knotting the horses' reins around a tree branch, Matt took Erin's hand in his and walked with her deeper into the pasture. They walked until they reached a small copse of trees surrounding a clearing. Erin stepped into the open space and sank down into the soft grass.

Without a word, Matt joined her. Stretching out beside her, he propped himself up on one elbow, his gaze never leaving Erin. She lay on her back, her arms folded beneath her head, gazing back at him with love-filled eyes. The scent of honeysuckle drifted on the air. One of the horses nickered, and Erin pulled her eyes away from Matt to look up at the millions of stars filling the sky.

"You ever seen anything like that?" she asked, her voice barely above a whisper.

"Not like this. It's beautiful," Matt agreed. "But it doesn't hold a candle to you."

Erin turned her head to look at him, at his eyes as they caught the faint glow of the moonlight. "It's why I love this place. No matter how hard things get, you look up at the sky, and it reminds you how small your problems are."

Matt reached out and brushed a strand of hair away from her face. "Your problems aren't small, Erin. But you're strong enough to handle them. You've proven that."

She rolled onto her side to face him. "I don't feel strong sometimes. Especially when I think about everything that's happened. Everything I've lost."

"You've also gained a lot," he said. "This ranch. The

people who care about you. A future where you can make a real difference."

His gaze held hers, and neither of them spoke for a moment. The air between them seemed to crackle with tension.

Erin finally broke the silence. "You were here through most of it. And now you're here again."

"I should have been here through all of it." He took her hand and brought it to his lips, kissing it softly.

"No. Everything happened the way it was meant to." She caressed his bottom lip with her thumb. "I needed to make the decision. I needed to confront my mother. And I needed to start the journey of Tranquil Trails. By myself. For myself." Erin's heart told her all this was true. But it also told her that now she was ready to share her life with the right person. And Matt was definitely that person. "But I'm glad you're back now."

"I wasn't going anywhere," he said. "Maybe we both just needed to wait for the right time."

She sat up, leaning closer to him, their fingers intertwining. "I don't know what I would've done without you, Matt."

He cupped her cheek, his thumb brushing lightly against her skin. "You're never going to find out."

Their kiss was slow and tentative at first, then deepened as months of tension and longing melted away. Erin's hands gripped his shirt as if he might disappear, and she wasn't about to let that happen.

They sank back into the grass together, and soon the warmth of his body against hers, the softness of his touch, the way she couldn't breathe when he kissed her neck consumed her.

The moon and the stars bore silent witness as Erin and Matt gave in to the pull they'd been denying for months. It was a moment of connection, of healing, of peace.

Just like Tranquil Trails.

When it was over, they lay tangled together in the grass. Erin rested her head on Matt's chest, her finger tracing a lazy pattern over his heart.

"I've never felt this safe," she said softly. "Even during the whole Alex thing—and you did make me feel safe then—somehow this feels different. Lasting."

"You deserve to feel safe." Matt kissed the top of her head. "And loved. Forever."

They stayed wrapped in each other's arms until even the breeze of a warm June night chilled them. They dressed and mounted the horses to ride back to the ranch house. As they rode side by side, Erin felt the bond between them deepen and strengthen even more, a quiet promise of a future they'd build together, one step at a time.

Epilogue

Boone County, Texas
Tranquil Trails Equine Therapy Ranch

The summer sun beat down on Tranquil Trails Equine Therapy Ranch as laughter and conversations filled the air. Erin had scheduled the grand opening for late afternoon, hoping to miss the worst of the July heat. But summer in Texas was what it was. She stood near the closest paddock with Angel, one of the therapy-trained horses she'd purchased a few weeks ago. The mare's ears flicked as a small child clambered onto her back with Erin's help.

"Hold tight to the reins, okay?" Erin adjusted the stirrups.

The little girl nodded, her face glowing with a wide grin as the horse whinnied. Holding the lead rope and staying alongside the saddle, Erin kept one arm looped around the child as they walked in circles. Within a few minutes, the girl was ready to get down and go play with her friends.

Erin tied Angel's lead to a hitching post and surveyed the crowd. She'd never expected this large of a gathering. Her heart warmed, knowing she owed it to her friends and neighbors.

People admired the newly built barn, now painted a warm red, the color Hank's old barn had been before it faded under the relentless Texas sun. It stood as the centerpiece of her vision, a testament to the hard work and generosity of everyone who had come together to make it a reality.

"Looking good out here, Erin." Nate Reed's booming voice drew her attention. He approached with his usual easy grin, a plate of food balanced in one hand.

Beside him, his wife, Sara, nodded in greeting. "I hear you've also fallen victim to the charms of a bodyguard." Her smile and wink made Erin laugh.

"Ah, yes. They do grow on you, don't they?" Erin glanced around, wondering where Matt had wandered off to. She noticed the rest of the Reed family standing near the fence, chatting. Their children ran in the grass, playing tag and chasing bubbles blown by—Detective Martinez? *That is one interesting woman.*

The Montgomerys' ranch foreman joined them. "This place... It's special. Hank would be proud."

Erin's throat tightened at the mention of Hank, but she managed a nod. "I hope so."

In the distance, children's laughter rang out as Erin's other new horse, Daisy, carried a young boy around the paddock, assisted by the new ranch therapist.

Just then, Matt appeared from around the corner of the house, his tool belt slung low on his hips. His T-shirt hugged his biceps and abs, and sawdust covered his forearms from the house renovations they'd been working on together. He caught Erin's eye and gave her a small smile that sent heat spiraling through her.

He sauntered over and greeted the others before turning to Erin. "Everything seems to be running smoothly."

Their eyes met, and for a moment, the people, the noise, the activity around them faded away. Matt reached out, brushing a stray strand of hair from her face. "You've done something amazing here, Erin," he murmured. "I'm so proud of you."

She gave a small laugh. "I had help."

His crystal-blue gaze steady, Matt said, "Still, this is your dream, and you made it real."

Before she could respond, another of the ranch hands from the Montgomerys' property approached. "Miss Erin, this place is incredible." He took his hat off and held it over his heart. "Hank… He'd be over the moon to see what you've done with his ranch."

Erin's chest tightened again, but this time with a mix of grief and gratitude. "Thank you," she said. "That means a lot."

The ranch hand nodded, setting his hat on his head again before walking off to join a group near the barn.

As the afternoon wore on, Erin watched the therapy horses work their quiet magic on the children, as well as a few teens and adults who ventured into the paddock. These people weren't even potential clients, yet the sense of peace and joy on their faces filled her with a deep sense of fulfillment. This was what she'd envisioned—a place of healing and connection.

After Matt had showered off the sawdust and changed clothes, he joined Erin. There if she needed him, but allowing her space to shine. She appreciated that as much as she did the frequent, loving glances he sent her way. But when all three of his bodyguard buddies kidnapped him for a beer, she wandered over to one of the long tables under a canopy, laden with food.

Erin greeted Brandon and Lisa Bauer, owners of her favorite barbecue place, with hugs. "I can't thank you enough for helping out like this." The Bauers had refused to accept a penny more than half price to cater her event.

"Are you kidding? Thank *you* for all the future business." Brandon spread his arms wide toward the crowd.

"Hopefully, we'll be doing more business together in the future." Erin leaned toward the couple. "You know darn well I won't be having any fancy-schmancy dining establishments cater my fundraisers."

"Damn straight," Lisa said. "And I'll bet those rich donors will be happy as hogs in mud when they're gnawing on rib bones and chugging beer."

Erin laughed at the visual, although she agreed. The guests at her parents' parties had always looked bored out of their minds.

Detective Martinez sauntered up to the barbecue spread and began loading a plate. "You've got quite the turnout," she said to Erin. "And quite the man, too."

Erin's eyes followed the detective's to where Matt helped a group of kids climbing on the paddock fence. "He's something else," she admitted, her lips curving into a smile.

Martinez chuckled. "Took you two long enough to figure it out."

Erin laughed softly, shaking her head. "It's been a journey, Detective. That's for sure."

As the sun began its descent, casting long shadows over the ranch, Erin gathered everyone near the barn. She stood on a small wooden platform, her hands clasped in front of her.

"Thank you all for being here today." Her voice was steady but full of emotion. "This ranch wouldn't be what it is without each and every one of you. Your support, your hard work, your belief in this dream, *my* dream, means everything to me."

She paused, her eyes scanning the crowd, hoping to see her parents but not expecting them. Despite most of the Montgomerys' ranch hands attending, her mother and father were clearly absent. But then she saw Maeve waving as she stood next to Liam in his wheelchair, a wide, crooked smile covering his face. A better surprise than even her parents.

"Hank believed in my dream and encouraged me to follow my heart. He believed in the power of horses to heal, to connect, just as I do. I hope Tranquil Trails can honor his memory and bring that same peace to everyone who comes here."

The crowd broke into applause, and tears pricked at the corners of Erin's eyes. As she stepped down from the platform, Matt was there, his hand outstretched. She took it, their fingers intertwining as he pulled her close.

"You did good," he said, his voice low.

"*We* did good." She leaned in and kissed him.

They stood together in the fading light, surrounded by friends and family, the promise of new beginnings woven into every corner of the ranch.

* * * * *

Get up to 4 Free Books!

We'll send you 2 free books from each series you try PLUS a free Mystery Gift.

FREE Value Over $25

Both the **Harlequin Intrigue®** and **Harlequin® Romantic Suspense** series feature compelling novels filled with heart-racing action-packed romance that will keep you on the edge of your seat.

YES! Please send me 2 FREE novels from the Harlequin Intrigue or Harlequin Romantic Suspense series and my FREE gift (gift is worth about $10 retail). After receiving them, if I don't wish to receive any more books, I can return the shipping statement marked "cancel." If I don't cancel, I will receive 6 brand-new Harlequin Intrigue Larger-Print books every month and be billed just $7.19 each in the U.S. or $7.99 each in Canada, or 4 brand-new Harlequin Romantic Suspense books every month and be billed just $6.39 each in the U.S. or $7.19 each in Canada, a savings of 20% off the cover price. It's quite a bargain! Shipping and handling is just 50¢ per book in the U.S. and $1.25 per book in Canada.* I understand that accepting the 2 free books and gift places me under no obligation to buy anything. I can always return a shipment and cancel at any time by calling the number below. The free books and gift are mine to keep no matter what I decide.

Choose one:
- ☐ **Harlequin Intrigue Larger-Print** (199/399 BPA G36Y)
- ☐ **Harlequin Romantic Suspense** (240/340 BPA G36Y)
- ☐ **Or Try Both!** (199/399 & 240/340 BPA G36Z)

Name (please print)

Address _____ Apt. #

City _____ State/Province _____ Zip/Postal Code

Email: Please check this box ☐ if you would like to receive newsletters and promotional emails from Harlequin Enterprises ULC and its affiliates. You can unsubscribe anytime.

Mail to the Harlequin Reader Service:
IN U.S.A.: P.O. Box 1341, Buffalo, NY 14240-8531
IN CANADA: P.O. Box 603, Fort Erie, Ontario L2A 5X3

Want to explore our other series or interested in ebooks? Visit www.ReaderService.com or call 1-800-873-8635.

---

*Terms and prices subject to change without notice. Prices do not include sales taxes, which will be charged (if applicable) based on your state or country of residence. Canadian residents will be charged applicable taxes. Offer not valid in Quebec. This offer is limited to one order per household. Books received may not be as shown. Not valid for current subscribers to the Harlequin Intrigue or Harlequin Romantic Suspense series. All orders subject to approval. Credit or debit balances in a customer's account(s) may be offset by any other outstanding balance owed by or to the customer. Please allow 4 to 6 weeks for delivery. Offer available while quantities last.

Your Privacy—Your information is being collected by Harlequin Enterprises ULC, operating as Harlequin Reader Service. For a complete summary of the information we collect, how we use this information and to whom it is disclosed, please visit our privacy notice located at https://corporate.harlequin.com/privacy-notice. Notice to California Residents – Under California law, you have specific rights to control and access your data. For more information on these rights and how to exercise them, visit https://corporate.harlequin.com/california-privacy. For additional information for residents of other U.S. states that provide their residents with certain rights with respect to personal data, visit https://corporate.harlequin.com/other-state-residents-privacy-rights/.

HIHRS25